Macbeth

– a novel –

PAUL ILLIDGE

Creber Monde

For Michael Milosh

Published by Creber Monde Entier
265 Port Union, 15-532
Toronto, ON M1C 4Z7 Canada
(416) 286-3988 1-866-631-4440 toll free
www.crebermonde.com

Distributed by Independent Publishers Group
814 North Franklin Street
Chicago, Illinois 60610 USA
(312) 337-0747 (312) 337-5985 fax
www.ipgbook.com
frontdesk@ipgbook.com

Design by Derek Chung Tiam Fook
Communications by JAG Business Services Inc.
Printed and bound in Canada by Hignell Book Printing, Winnipeg, Manitoba

Library and Archives Canada Cataloguing in Publication

Illidge, Paul
Macbeth / prose translation by Paul Illidge.

(The Shakespeare novels)
ISBN 0-9686347-2-9

I. Shakespeare, William, 1564-1616 Macbeth.
II. Title. III. Series: Illidge, Paul Shakespeare novels.

PR2878.M3I45 2006   C813'.54   C2006-901468-X

Macbeth

Text of the First Folio 1623

Characters

Duncan	*King of Scotland*
Donalbain	
Malcolm	*his sons*

Macbeth	
Banquo	*generals of the King's army*

Macduff	
Lenox	
Rosse	
Menteth	*noblemen of Scotland*
Angus	
Caithness	

Fleance	*son of Banquo*
Siward	*Earl of Northumberland, English general*
Young Siward	*his son*
Seyton	*an officer attending Macbeth*
Boy	*son of Macduff*
English Doctor	
Scottish Doctor	
Soldier	
Porter	
Old Man	
Three Men	
Soldier Bandits	
Lady Macbeth	
Lady Macduff	
Gentlewoman	
Hecate	
Three Witches	

Lords, Gentlemen, Officers, Soldiers, Attendants, Messengers
Ghost of Banquo, Apparitions, Spirits

A summer storm moves on over the barren and deserted countryside of Scotland during the early Middle Ages, leaving the rain-soaked fields cloaked in clouds of fog.

While the sound of thunder fades in the distant sky, stray flashes of lightning illuminate the ghostly white faces of three witches who are huddled around a black cauldron suspended over a fire that is about to go out.

Their ragged clothes barely covering the nakedness of their bone-thin bodies, they stare at the hissing fire, all three with the same sea-blue eyes, until one witch, whose hoary gray beard almost touches the ground, leans in with a meager stick and pokes at the smoldering ashes in the fire. The second witch, a twin of the first and similarly long bearded, her hands and forearms red as though they've been dipped in blood, picks up the stump of a human leg and gives the liquid inside the cauldron a good stir. The third witch, whose face is nose-less but has nostrils, suddenly grows agitated and starts rolling her head around on her shoulders, wringing her sharp-nailed hands together in her lap.

"*When shall we three meet again?*" the first witch sings in a child's soft voice, "*in thunder, lightning, or in rain?*"

"*When the battle's finally done,*" the second witch sings in a voice identical to her sister's, "*one side having lost, the other having won.*"

" *– Which will precede the setting sun,*" the third witch sings, in the stern voice of an older woman.

"And where might we three be just then?"

"Again upon the barren heath."

"There to meet the man Macbeth," the third witch declares as she stops rolling her head, stands up and heads off across the soggy field.

"I'm coming Graymalkin!"

"And Paddock too!"

The two twins shuffle along behind the third witch.

"Until then!" the third witch pronounces.

The three women trudge slowly into the fog, chanting playfully as they go: *"Fair is foul and foul is fair. Hover in fog and filthy air..."*

The fields near Forres thick with fog, an urgent burst of bugles sounds the arrival within the army camp of Duncan, King of Scotland, as he slows his horse to a walk and signals his two sons Malcolm and Donalbain, the noble Lord Lenox, and a retinue of soldiers, attendants and banner bearers, to do the same. All are muddy and bleeding from wounds to the face and body. All have the look of defeat in their faces, King Duncan especially worried when he sees the steady stream of stretchers, carts and wagons arriving back in camp with casualties from the battlefield.

A soldier bleeding badly from wounds to his stomach and legs, slips in the mud but gets up and staggers bravely towards the King.

"What poor fellow is this?" Duncan asks his sons. "He might have news of how the rebellion stands…"

" – This is the sergeant who saved me from being captured," Malcolm points out. "Hail, brave friend!" he calls to the soldier. "Tell the King what the situation was when you left the battlefield."

The sergeant nods. "Things could have gone either way," he explains dutifully, wincing with the pain of his wounds. "Both sides were like exhausted swimmers clinging to each other for dear life, when the traitor Macdonwald – in true rebel fashion, heaping evil upon evil – brought forward reinforcements of infantry and axmen he had recruited, unbeknownst to us, in the Western shires. Suddenly outnumbered, it looked like victory was going to be his after all, because we were just too weak by then – when Macbeth took up his sword and, not caring of the consequences, carved his way straight through enemy lines as though he had turned executioner, until he was face to face with Macdonwald, and without a word of greeting or farewell, he slit the traitor from crotch to chin, lopped off his head and stuck it on the tip of our battle flag."

"Oh valiant cousin! Worthiest of men!" Duncan exclaims.

"As happens when the sun breaks through after a bad storm, we thought the tide had turned, and it had, but not in our favor. Believe me, your Majesty, believe me, no sooner had the forces fighting for our noble cause sent the peasant hordes into retreat, than the Norwegian commander saw his opportunity and with fresh supplies of weapons and men launched a new attack against us."

"Were not our captains Macbeth and Banquo disheartened by this?" Duncan asks.

"As sparrows are before eagles, rabbits before lions," the sergeant smiles weakly "but I can truly report that they exploded like twice-charged cannons in the numerous blows they inflicted for every one the enemy tried to land, as if they meant to bathe in the blood of wounds they were giving out, or sought to turn the field into another Golgotha, it was hard to tell which – but I'm hurt badly, Sire – my wounds need tending – "

"Your wounds and your words both do you credit. Get him to the surgeons!" Duncan orders, noticing a horseman riding through the camp toward him. "Who comes here?"

"The worthy Thane of Rosse," Malcolm says.

"He seems in a great hurry, as if he has important news," Lenox observes.

"God save the King," Rosse says, greeting Duncan.

"From whence have you come, worthy Thane?"

"From Fife, your majesty, where the Norwegian forces struck fear in our troops because of their vast numbers. Sweno, the King of Norway, together with the Thane of Cawdor who had betrayed you, sire, and gone over to the enemy side, began a punishing attack that wreaked havoc on our men. But only until they were confronted by Macbeth, who faced them with courage defiant, and with valor rather than treachery spurring him on, went after Sweno and Cawdor like Mars the god of war himself, fighting hand to hand in brute battle until the Norwegian was overpowered, Cawdor fled, and victory fell to us – "

"This is wonderful happiness!" Duncan rejoices.

" – Sweno requested a peace treaty at once, however we refused even to let him bury his dead until he met us at Inchcomb and paid a rich bounty for supporting Cawdor's revolt."

"The Thane of Cawdor will betray us no more," Duncan declares solemnly and turns to Rosse. "Go and see he is put to death, and give his title to noble Macbeth."

"I'll see it done."

"What he has lost, Macbeth has won…" His spirits buoyed by the news he's just received, Duncan smiles to himself as he gives the order for his sons and followers to proceed the rest of the way into camp. He glances at the sky once they are moving: the rain has started again.….

The first witch stands beside an ancient-looking rock cairn not far from the cart path that runs through the bottom of a highland valley. The enormous boulders that form the top of the cairn have been worn smooth and round over time. Slipping a finger into the lower part of her hoary beard, the first witch brings out a roasted chestnut, which she splits open against the side of a rock and eats. Chewing her food, she hears a squeal of laughter from behind the cairn. She moves hastily around to the other side and sees her bearded twin struggling toward the cairn with the third witch on her back.

"Where have you been?" the first witch calls.

"Killing pigs," the second witch pants, then runs the last few steps to the cairn and groans in relief as she sets her passenger down.

Meanwhile the first witch has turned and found a gap in the rocks that she squeezes through to go inside the cairn. As thunder sounds in the dreary sky overhead, the other witches follow suit.

In a few moments the three of them emerge from an opening atop the cairn and, after embracing, sit down facing each other.

"And you, sister?" the third witch asks.

"A sailor's wife had chestnuts in her lap," the first witch explains, "and munched, and munched, and munched. 'Give me some,' I said. 'Go to hell, witch!' the fat-bottomed sow yelled back. Her husband had sailed east to Syria, captain of a ship called 'The Tiger'. So in a boat full of holes I will make my way there. And like a rat without a tail I'll spin, I'll spin, I'll spin!"

"I'll give you some wind."

"You are too kind."

"And I some too."

"I myself will this then do: the wind from every port will blow, wherever the ship's map has him go. I'll drain him till he's dry as hay, keep him thirsty night and day. Never sleeping, that is the worst, for any soul we three have cursed. Weary weeks at sea he will moan, longing for just a sight of home. But never will his ship be lost; I'll keep it forever on the tempest tossed. Look what I have," she grins.

"Show me, show me," the second witch pleads.

The first witch reaches into her beard again. She holds what she pulls out in a closed fist then unclenches her fingers to show them something fleshy pink, small and bloody in the palm of her hand. "A captain's thumb, lopped as homeward he did come!"

Looking gleefully at the severed thumb, the third witch glances up suddenly, jumps to her feet and strains to hear the beat of a marching drum approaching in the distance. "A drum!" she cries, "a drum! Macbeth has come!"

The other witches are on their feet promptly, all three joining hands and chanting together: "Three weird sisters, hand in hand – traveling fast on sea or land, thus will dance around, around – "

"Three times yours!" the first witch calls.

"And three times mine!" the second one says.

"And three again to make it nine!" the third sister adds.

"Shh!" they suddenly whisper in unison. "The spell is done – "

They scurry back to the opening in the rocks from whence they came and descend into the cairn only a moment before several cracks of thunder shatter the stillness of the valley and a hard rain begins to fall. . .

Their horses rearing in fear of the sudden thunder, Macbeth and

Banquo struggle briefly with the animals until they have them moving forward again along the cart path through the valley, two columns of soldiers marching behind the warrior generals in time to the drummer's steady beat: *doom, doom, duh-doom-doom-doom.*

"I've not seen weather change from fair to foul as quickly as it has today," Macbeth says, pulling up the hood of his cloak.

Banquo nods, covering his head against the downpour as well. "How far is Forres from here?"

But his attention suddenly on something up ahead, Macbeth doesn't answer. Banquo quickly puts up his hand and orders the column to halt. He follows Macbeth's pointing finger, straining his eyes to see through the teeming rain until he too notices the three female figures standing in the middle of the cart path: their blue eyes shimmering, the tattered bits of clothing they wear over their bony, misshapen bodies offering no protection from the pelting rain. Two have beards down to their ankles; one has nostrils without a nose.

"What are these things, so hideous and strange they look not human, yet appear to be. Are you alive?" Banquo demands, "can you hear me?" He turns to Macbeth. "The way they're putting fingers to their lips tells me they understand." He addresses the witches again. "You appear to be women and yet your beards persuade me you can't be! What are you?"

"Speak, if you can!" Macbeth calls. "What are you?"

The first witch takes her finger away from her lips. "All hail, Macbeth! Hail to you, Thane of Glamis!"

The second witch repeats her sister's motion. "All hail, Macbeth! Hail to you, Thane of Cawdor!"

"All hail, Macbeth, who will be King before long!" the third witch proclaims.

Unable to stop looking at the third witch, who bows repeatedly before him, Macbeth is perplexed and bewildered.

"Good sir," Banquo says, "why are you taken aback when better news than this you could never hope to hear? – Give us the truth, are you creations of fantasy or human, as you appear to be?" The witches remain silent, the bearded twins watching as the third witch continues bowing.

"My noble partner you greet with the title he presently holds," Banquo shouts, "with the greatness of another that you predict will be his, along with the prospect of royal ascension. He is duly and powerfully entranced – yet of me you will not speak. If indeed you can glimpse the future, say what will happen and what will not, speak to me as well, who neither begs your favor nor fears your hate."

"Hail!"

"Hail!"

"Hail!"

"Lesser than Macbeth," the first witch says, "but greater."

"Not so happy, yet much happier," says the second.

"You will have kings, though not be one yourself," the third witch concludes. "So all hail, Macbeth and Banquo!"

"Banquo – "

"And Macbeth – "

"All hail!" the third witch says, takes the other two by the hand and begins walking backwards away from the soldiers, disappearing almost immediately in the heavy rain.

"Wait, mysterious speakers, tell me more!" Macbeth cries, jumping down from his horse to go after them. He charges through the rain, straining his eyes to locate them…but they are gone. "On my father's death I became Thane of Glamis," he shouts over the sound of the drumming rain, "but how can I be Thane of Cawdor when he is alive and well? And to be King is less believable than to be Cawdor – yet tell me from whence these tidings come – why you have stopped us on our way with such prophecies? – Speak, I command you!"

As if the sound of his voice has done something, the rain suddenly diminishes and within a moment has stopped altogether. The valley begins to fill with afternoon sunlight.

Banquo bringing up his horse, Macbeth remounts.

"The earth can trick the eye as water does," Banquo offers, handing him the reins to his horse. "These were such a thing – or else where did they vanish to?"

"Into thin air," says Macbeth, his eyes taking in the deserted fields around them.

"Their bodies were here, yet they melted away as breath does in wind. I wish they had stayed…"

Banquo shrugs. "But were they truly here, or did we lose our thinking for a time and but mistake them as living things?"

They start riding again.

"Your sons shall be kings," Macbeth says.

"But you shall be King," Banquo comes back with a smile.

"And Thane of Cawdor too, did they not say so?"

Banquo regards Macbeth. "Their very words…" As he finishes speaking he catches sight of horsemen galloping toward them, flags of the King of Scotland flying red and gold on their standards.

The noblemen Rosse and Angus slow their horses to a canter as they reach the cart path and ride up to join Banquo and Macbeth at the head of the marching column.

Rosse is the first to speak. "The King rejoices at the news of your success, Macbeth, and hearing of your personal bravery in the face of a much stronger rebel force, his admiration competes with his praise as to what he should thank you for first: in short, he is speechless. Even more, when later in the day he learned how you charged into the midst of Norway's finest armor, yet with your men dying all around you had no fear for yourself at all. Messengers came to the king one after another, each report commending your actions defending his Majesty."

"He has sent us to convey his deep gratitude and to bring you before him."

"*We* are not to reward you," Rosse smiles at Macbeth, "but as a pledge toward future honors, I am ordered to address you as Thane of Cawdor, and am pleased to do so: Hail, most worthy Thane of Cawdor, for such is now your title."

"What!" Banquo says to himself, "can the Devil speak the truth?"

"The Thane of Cawdor lives," Macbeth protests. "Why do you dress me in someone else's clothes?"

"The man who was Cawdor lives still, " Angus explains, "but he is sentenced to death and rightly so. I know not whether he joined forces with Norway, was secretly in league with the rebels, or was even working with both to overthrow the King. But he has confessed to treason, it has been proved, his life and lands are forfeit."

"Glamis, now Thane of Cawdor too," Macbeth murmurs to himself, looking away from the others as they ride along, "and the greatest prediction still to come." He turns to Rosse and Angus who have fallen in behind the two generals. "Thanks both, for your trouble," he says heartily, just as Banquo catches his eye and points out the sun's position low in the western sky. Macbeth nods in agreement with what has to be done. He gives orders for the column to step up the pace. Shouts pass loudly down the line and within moments the drummer has promptly quickened his marching beat: *doom, doom, duh-doom-doom-doom...*

As they move along, Macbeth throws Banquo a knowing look. "Don't you now look forward to your children being kings, since those who brought me Cawdor's title promised nothing less to you?"

"May be," he replies, as though the matter is neither here nor there with him, "but taking their words to heart could easily excite your desire to be King as well as Cawdor." He pauses before continuing. "What happened before was passing strange, yet often the powers of darkness win us over by tempting us with things we would like to be true. They gain our trust in small ways first, only to betray us later, when the stakes are much higher," he warns. Macbeth acknowledges Banquo's words, watches his partner fall back for a word with Rosse and Angus about a different matter.

"Two things I was told have come true," Macbeth remarks quietly, not wanting to be overheard, "which sets the scene for a royal drama in which I could become King..."

Listening to Banquo's flattering description of Macbeth in battle, Rosse and Angus offer their enthusiastic compliments.

"Thank you, gentlemen," he acknowledges evenly, but returns quickly to his own private thoughts. "Such supernatural tempting cannot be evil. If it is, why have I been led to believe my future success by the first prophecy coming so quickly true? I have been made Thane of Cawdor. Yet, if good, then why in my mind's eye do I now see images so horrid that, against my very nature, they make my hair stand on end and my heart pound in my chest? It must be that horrors imagined are worse than fears which confront us here and now. Though the act of murder is merely a thought, it shakes me to my very core and the power to think clearly is clouded over with wild imaginings, so that only they seem real…"

"The Thane of Cawdor drifts in deep contemplation," Banquo jokes with Rosse and Angus, but Macbeth shows no reaction.

" – If fortune means to make me King, then fortune may crown me without my having to do a thing…"

"New honors are like new clothes to him," Banquo says in a louder voice this time, "they fit better once they've been worn in."

" – Whatever comes to be, the roughest day will pass like any other…"

"Worthy Macbeth," Banquo calls forward, "We wait upon your decision…"

"I beg your pardon: my dull brain was recalling things I had forgotten. Kind gentlemen, your efforts are recorded here," he taps a finger against his temple. "Indeed, they are written down so that each day I can read them anew. – Let us go and meet the King!"

As Banquo rides up beside him, Macbeth glances over. "Think about what we have seen and heard, Banquo. And when there has been time to reflect on what has happened, let us speak to one another…"

"Most gladly," Banquo replies.

"Enough, then. – Come, friends!" Macbeth calls to Rosse and Angus. He gives the signal to begin a quick march and in a moment the drummer doubles his beat to speed the column toward King Duncan's castle at Forres: *doom-duh-duh, doom-duh-duh, doom-doom-doom….*

The gold and red flags of the King of Scotland flap in the stiff breeze atop Forres Castle, Duncan and his son Malcolm looking down from the ramparts as Macbeth's soldiers make camp outside the castle walls after their journey. Amid the sound of axes chopping firewood and mallets pounding tent pegs, the words "Cawdor" and "traitor" figure prominently in the chatter that drifts upward within range of the King's hearing. Before long, Duncan steps back from the wall and turns abruptly to his son. "Has the execution taken place?" he asks brusquely, and starts walking along the upper platform, sentries coming to attention as he passes. "And those in charge, have they returned yet?"

"No, father, they are not back," Malcolm answers, "but I've spoken with someone who saw him die," he hastens to add as he follows his father down the rooftop stairs. "The man reported that Cawdor freely admitted his treason, beseeched your Highness' pardon, and declared himself deeply sorry for what he had done." Inside the castle, they move through a torch-lit hall before descending more stairs. "Nothing in his life quite became the manner in which he died," Malcolm goes on. "According to the witness, he left this world like one who had for some time been practicing how to do away with the most precious thing he owned, as if it meant nothing to lose his life."

"There is no way of telling what someone is thinking by the look on his face," Duncan says firmly. "Cawdor was someone whom I trusted completely."

Rounding a corner, they make their way along a corridor that widens at the entrance to the throne room, where an entourage is waiting: the King's other son, Donalbain, the noble Lenox, numerous dignitaries, officials and attendants. Duncan acknowledges them with a brief nod and moves straight into the throne room.

A flourish of trumpets signaling the arrival of the King, he enters the room but breaks away from the procession almost immediately in order to greet Macbeth, who is standing near the throne alongside Rosse, Angus and Banquo.

"Oh worthiest cousin!" Duncan exclaims. "I was feeling terribly ungrateful just now because my gratitude can't keep pace with the swiftness of your actions on my behalf. You are accomplishing so much at every turn that thanks and reward are slow to catch up with you." The King's humor prompts mild laughter around the room. "All I can say, is that you are due much more than can ever be paid."

"Being able to serve you is payment in itself, sire," Macbeth responds. "Your Highness' part is only to receive our loyalty: we are children and servants in our duty to your Majesty and the throne. Doing all we can to protect the King we love and honor is merely doing what faithful subjects should," he declares, and bows again.

"Welcome to Forres," Duncan says warmly, taking Macbeth aside. "I have planted you here," he confides, putting a hand to his heart, "and I will do all I can to see you flourish. – Noble Banquo, no less deserving of our praise, nor less of seeing what you have done made known to all, let me embrace you and hold you to my heart."

"There let me be, and all that I am be your own."

Embracing Banquo, the King steps toward the throne and has Malcolm stand beside him. An emotional moment, he takes his son's hand and begins to speak, his voice filled with emotion. "I confess my many plentiful joys this day have me feeling close to tears. For let it be known sons, kinsmen, Thanes and all who are close to my heart, that on my death the kingdom shall pass to my eldest son, Malcolm, who as my heir will now bear the title Prince of Cumberland." A cheer of congratulation resounds throughout the room. "Yet honor is not being bestowed on him alone," the King continues. "The light of royal favor and reward will also shine on all who are deserving." The announcement prompts another rousing cheer. "From here, let us travel to the castle of Macbeth at Inverness, where we may further strengthen the bonds that are between us." As cheers salute this last decree, Duncan brings Malcolm over to Macbeth and they embrace.

"It is more work when I am not serving you, sire," Macbeth addresses Duncan, "so, grant that I be the messenger to give my wife the joyful news of your intended visit."

"Indeed, worthy Thane," Duncan nods, agreeing to the request.

" – And so I take my humble leave." Macbeth bows to the King and to Malcolm before turning to leave.

"My worthy Cawdor!" Duncan calls after him, a signal for more cheering.

Once outside the throne room, Macbeth turns and gazes resentfully at the King as he presents Malcolm to Banquo and the other assembled nobles. "The Prince of Cumberland!" he murmurs bitterly. "This is an obstacle which stands directly in my path – it could foil me in this business altogether unless I can find a way to leap over him." He pauses for a moment, running the matter over in his mind. "Stars, hide your fires, so their light will not see my dark and secret desires," he says menacingly, "even as I turn a blind eye to what my hand must do: for when it is done, it can't help but be what every eye fears to see…"

" – True, worthy Banquo!" Duncan smiles in the throne room, his arm around Banquo's shoulder. "He is every bit as brave as you say. It warms my heart to hear you sing his praises – it is music to my ears. Let's follow our peerless kinsman as he goes before to prepare a welcome for us."

As Banquo moves to make way for those crowding eagerly around Malcolm and the King, he catches a glimpse of Macbeth standing at the door, looking on.…

Its rider slouching exhausted in the saddle, a black stallion continues at full gallop as it leaves the forest road behind and races across the hillside meadow toward the gray stone towers of Inverness Castle, flags of the Thane of Glamis ruffling slightly in the late-morning breeze. Within moments, a sentry atop the castle walls gives word, and soon the great wooden doors begin to open.

Standing in her nightgown at the window of her tower room, Lady Macbeth takes brief notice of the approaching horseman, but turns anxiously back to a letter she has been reading: "…They met me on the day we defeated the rebels, and those who are informed about such things tell me that their knowledge extends beyond our mortal realm. I was mad to question them further but they vanished into thin air before my very eyes. While I stood staring in amazement, messengers happened to arrive from the King, and they hailed me not only as Thane of Glamis but of Cawdor too – the very titles with which these Weird Sisters had addressed me, along with the words 'Hail, Macbeth, who shall be King hereafter!' I wanted you to know this, my dearest partner in greatness, so that you could rightly rejoice knowing the greatness that lies before you as well – though you must keep this to yourself. Farewell.'"

She glances up from the letter, her face strangely empty of joy. "You are Glamis, and now Cawdor, and are bound to be what you have been promised. But I fear your nature is too much filled with striving after goodness to do what will be necessary now – you wish for greatness and you are ambitious for it, but you lack the ruthless will that makes it possible. You crave high position but you would have it by the moral book. You would not deceive to get what you desire and yet you would welcome it if it came to you unfairly. The truth is, great Glamis, the act which cries 'This must be done to gain the crown', is one I know you are afraid to do, though neither would you like it left undone…" Setting the letter down on the writing table before her, she gazes out the window again. "Get here quickly, so that I may give you those words of courage and conviction you will need to overcome the fears that stand between you and the golden crown, which fate and her magic sisters seem to have promised will be yours – "

A hard knock at the door causes her to start. She moves quickly across the room, suspicious of whoever is there.

"What is your news?" she calls warily.

"The King is coming here tonight," a man's voice replies.

"You are mad to say so!" Lady Macbeth protests, darting to her bedside table where she picks up a key from beside a plate of food that hasn't been touched. "Isn't your Master with him?" she asks as she hurries back to the door, her hands shaking badly while she fumbles violently with the key until the door swings open. She gestures curtly for the messenger to enter. "If the King were coming, your Master would have sent me a message so I could prepare," she scolds. She closes the door behind him and relocks it.

"With all respect, madam, it is true: our Thane is arriving. A fellow has come ahead to inform you, so exhausted it was all he could do to deliver his message."

Lady Macbeth offers a contrite smile. "Give him good care, then. He brings great news."

The messenger bows, turns to go, and waits patiently while Lady Macbeth lets him out.

When he is gone she walks over and sits down on the edge of her bed. She remains motionless for a moment, then folds her hands primly in her lap and looks down at them, tenderly. "The raven will croak himself hoarse during Duncan's fatal arrival under my roof," she says, as if there's someone in the room to whom she's talking. She shuts her eyes and begins opening and closing her hands. "Come, you spirits that nurture deadly thoughts," she prays, her hands working faster, "unsex me here and fill me from head to toe until my very being overflows with vile cruelty! Thicken my blood and stop up the holes in which remorse could enter me so conscience cannot come between my deadly plan and its effect. Come then to my breasts," she pants, "and have my milk turn bitter, you makers of murder, wherever in your secret spheres you wait for Nature's havoc to begin! Come, thick night, and shroud yourself in Hell's dark smoke so my sharp knife will never see the wound it makes, and Heaven will not dare to peep through the blanket of the dark, to cry, 'Stop, stop!'"

There are voices in the hall. Lady Macbeth glances over, her face brightening as she hears someone trying the door. She moves off the bed and hurries to open up.

"Great Glamis!" she cries when he steps into the room, "worthy Cawdor! And soon to be hailed greater than both!" She embraces him, then lifts her head and says, smiling, "Your letters have carried me away from this dull present so I can feel our very future even now."

"Duncan comes here tonight, my dearest love," he says, watching her cross to the writing table by the window, strewn with quill pens, sealing wax and ink-spattered, half-written letters.

She picks up the one from him she was reading. "How long will he be staying?"

"He says until tomorrow."

Taking a candle whose holder is a mound of melted wax, she puts a corner of the letter into the flame and turns to him as it ignites. "Never will he see the light of day," she says coldly, staring at the last bit of paper until the flame burns too close and she lets go, the cinder floating to the floor.

Macbeth looks uneasily at her.

"Your face, my Thane, is like a book which any man may read and know upon the instant what thoughts turn there. To deceive the world you must see yourself as the world does: with welcoming warmth in your eye, your hand, your tongue. Look like you are the innocent flower, while beneath, you are being the serpent. We must receive our guest as custom fits, but you must put tonight's great business into my hands so in all the days and nights to come, ours will be the power in this fair kingdom."

"We will speak further," he says and abruptly turns.

Lady Macbeth quickly takes him by the arm. "Look as though your conscience is clear," she warns. "Be calm and composed, and you have nothing to fear…"

She moves to kiss him, but he turns and heads for the door.

" – And leave the rest to me, my dear!" she calls after him….

The late day sun casts a rich, golden light over the countryside as Duncan and his men arrive at Inverness castle, the King stopping his horse and turning in the saddle to gaze back over the green valley through which they've just come.

"This castle is perfectly situated," he remarks keenly, " the air so fresh and sweet to the senses."

Banquo nods, steadying his horse beside the King. "The swallows usually live under the eaves of churches during summer," Banquo explains, "but it seems they've taken up residence here on this castle." He points to the upper walls and roof, "No buttress, frieze or outward cornice is without one of their hanging nests – which means the air must be specially pleasant if they choose to live and breed here."

Duncan closes his eyes and savors the cool air a final time, then, facing front again, he proceeds through the great wooden doors to the castle's inner yard, which instantly becomes noisy with activity. Musicians on lute, recorder and tabor drum begin to play; pages, servants and stable boys rush to take charge of the visitors' horses and tend the wagons drawing up behind. Malcolm and Donalbain, the King's sons, along with Banquo, Lenox, Macduff, Rosse and Angus, follow Duncan as he advances to greet Lady Macbeth.

"Look here – our fair hostess," he says to the others, receiving her respectful curtsey. "The love of our subjects is sometimes a burden," he confides as she rises, "but we are ever thankful, for where would we be without it?" he asks, smiling. "I only say this to let you know how grateful we are for your trouble and the love it shows."

"If everything we have done for you were doubled and doubled again, it would rank a pittance against the great and generous rewards, both past and present, which your Majesty has seen fit to bestow upon us – and for which you will always have a place in our prayers."

"Where is the Thane of Cawdor?" Duncan inquires. "We followed right behind him from Forres and had hoped to arrive ahead of him, but he rides fast. And with his great love for you spurring him on," he says with a flattering smile, "he has reached here first. Fair and noble hostess, we are your guests tonight."

"Ever your servants, we owe all we have, we are and may become, to your Highness, and are therefore happy to put ourselves at your Majesty's disposal in return for these gracious favors."

Touched by her gratitude, Duncan reaches for her hand, kisses it, and then keeps it affectionately between both of his. "Show me to our host," he says as he begins walking. "We revere Macbeth greatly and welcome this opportunity to show our pleasure toward him. Lead the way, madam…"

Lady Macbeth heads Duncan toward the castle entrance, his sons and noble entourage falling in behind, Banquo the only one to notice dozens of cheeping swallows fleeing their nests along the castle walls high overhead….

There is great coming and going outside the hall in which Macbeth and his wife are entertaining Duncan, his noble friends, their knights and followers. Servants holding plates and platters heaped with steaming fish, roasted fowl and sizzling beef, are assembling under the watchful eye of the castle's chief steward, who is fit to be tied because the musician playing the lute has just broken a string. The tabor player offers to find another instrument and tosses his drum to the steward so the frantic man has no choice but to catch it, just as Macbeth comes from the hall to see why the food is not being served. The steward quickly orders the servant train to make ready, the tabor player returning with another lute and taking back his drum. Macbeth nods to the steward and he starts people moving into the hall, the musicians striking up a tune to accompany the procession, only Macbeth remaining behind.

Moving to the door, he stops before going in and gazes across the tables and benches lined with soldiers swilling ale, their laughter turning to cheers as the banquet feast is laid before the King.

"If it could be over with once it is done, then it would be best to see it done quickly: if the murder could be the end of it, and his death the culmination of my hopes in a single blow, here and now, once and for all, then who wouldn't risk the life to come?" He ponders the thought. "But we are punished in this world for our deeds in this world – advise strong measures, yet, being accepted, they come back to be used against us: even-handed justice brings the very drink we've poisoned up to our own lips. The King trusts me for two great reasons. First, I am his kinsman and his subject, both strong arguments against the deed. Second, I am his host, the one to shut the door against his murderer, not wield the killing weapon myself. Duncan has, as well, ruled with such kindness and generosity that his virtues will cause a clamor loud as angels' trumpet blasts in protest against the great evil of his murder. And Pity, like a newborn babe riding the wind, or infant angels mounted upon invisible currents of air, will blow the horrible deed into every living eye so that tears will fall like rain. – No, the only cause I have to want this done is my ambition to grow in greatness, which, leaping too high, could miss what it strives to grasp, and fall the other way – "

He breaks off when Lady Macbeth comes through the door to speak with him.

"And so, what news?"

"He is busy with his feast. Why did you leave the room?"

"Has he asked for me?"

"You know very well he has."

He stares off. "We will go no further with this," he says. "The King has honored me of late and I have won the trusting admiration of a great many people. These things deserve to be enjoyed at their full, not discarded so soon."

Lady Macbeth reacts instantly. "Were you drunk when you spoke of the greatness that awaits us? Have you been asleep since then and are now just waking, sick at the thought of what you so freely expressed? Henceforth I will know the true value of your love. Are you afraid to be as brave in your actions as you are in your desires? Would you have the crown that you prize above everything else, yet know you are a coward at heart, who let 'I will do this' make way for 'I dare not' – like the cat in the proverb who wanted fish but was afraid to get his feet wet?"

"Please, peace. I dare do anything a man should do. Who dares do more is more beast, than man – "

"What beast was it then, that made you break this news to me at all? You were a man when you dared to talk of doing it, and you would be so much more the man if you made your talking into doing. Neither time nor the place was ready before, and yet you were happy to plan for both: and now that things have fallen into place, that very falling scares the courage in you away. I have been a nursing mother, and know how sweet it is to love the child upon my breast. But I would, while the babe was smiling up at me, have plucked my nipple from its toothless mouth and dashed its brains on rock if I had sworn to you I would, as you have sworn to me of killing the King."

Macbeth meets her eyes. "But what if we should fail?"

"We fail? Just keep your courage at the ready point and we will not fail. When Duncan is asleep – which his hard day's journey will send him heavily to – I will make the guards outside his room so drunk from toasting the King they won't remember a thing. Dead to the world and snoring like pigs, what cannot you and I do to the dreaming Duncan? What have his drunken protectors accused of, but guilt for our great murder?"

"Bear male-children only," Macbeth says, amazed, "for such cold blood is made to fill the veins of men alone." He takes her words and thinks them through. "When we have used their daggers and then smeared with blood their clothes and hands, will it not be thought that they have done the deed?"

"How could one believe it otherwise, since we shall wail in grief and woe with all the rest on hearing of his death?"

"I am ready, and strain with all my strength unto this deed. Let us go, and have deceiving looks a pleasant purpose show: false faces must hide what false hearts know."

Hours later, a torch flickers high in one of the castle's upper archways and soon goes out. Quiet and still, moments pass in darkness until, with a sound of shuffling footsteps, Banquo's son Fleance arrives, carrying a freshly lit torch. His first night on guard duty, he removes the burnt torch and mounts the new one in its place. He blows on his hands to keep them warm, stepping over to the balustrade that gives onto the inner courtyard. Head back, he gazes up at the black, starless night – when someone comes from behind and puts a hand on his shoulder.

"What time is it?"

Fleance turns at the sound of the voice, frightened but trying not to appear that way, and sees with relief that it's his father, Banquo. "The moon is down, sir, and I haven't heard the clock chime," Fleance reports.

"The moon goes down at midnight," Banquo says mildly, smiling at the serious effort his son is giving his guard duties.

"It must be later then, sir.

"And you, sir?" Banquo asks and casts a teasing look at his son's uniform.

Fleance glances down, then sheepishly back at his father. He has no weapon.

"Take my sword," Banquo says, unbuckling and handing over his. While Fleance dons the sword, Banquo approaches the balustrade and looks out into the darkness.

"They're thrifty in heaven on nights like this, with all their lights out," he jokes. "Take this too," he says and removes his dagger belt.

When Fleance has trouble adjusting the weapons around his waist, Banquo squats and helps him. " ...My eyes keep closing, but I can't drift off," he complains, while he works to make the belt fit. "If only the Powers that be could keep away the bad dreams which come to me when I sleep – " A sudden noise brings him to his feet and he breaks off. "Give me the sword," he whispers. Fleance quickly draws and passes it over. "Who's there?" Banquo demands.

"A friend," Macbeth answers before stepping into the torch's light. He acknowledges Fleance with a nod then reaches out and clenches fists with Banquo.

"Yet awake, sir?"

Macbeth nods, watching as Banquo returns his sword to Fleance."The King's gone to bed. He was in an unusually good mood tonight, and showed great largesse in his gifts to your household. Why, that diamond he presented to your wife for her hospitality..." He whistles in admiration. "Well, he went off to bed highly contented," Banquo says.

"We weren't expecting him," Macbeth points out, "and so we weren't able to entertain him quite the way we would have liked."

"I thought it went well," Banquo remarks after a prolonged silence, noticing the troubled look that has entered Macbeth's face. "I do have dreams of the three Weird Sisters," Banquo offers. "I had one again last night..." When Macbeth doesn't answer, Banquo continues talking. "Some of what they told you has come true, has it not?"

"I don't think about them," Macbeth says dismissively, aware that Fleance is listening. "Yet when I can find the time I'd like to speak with you about that business, in some spare moment perhaps."

"Whenever you are free, sir..."

Macbeth lowers his voice. "If you will go along with me when the time is right, you would receive new honors."

"So long as I would lose none that are mine now by trying to win more, nor break my clear conscience, nor change my loyalty to the King, I could be accepting of advice," Banquo answers tactfully.

"In the meantime, sleep well, sir."

"The same to you, general."

Coming to attention, Fleance properly salutes Macbeth and follows his father back inside.

When the sound of their footsteps has receded, Macbeth signals a servant who has waited behind him in the shadows. "Go and tell my lady to ring the bell when my drink is ready." He approaches the balustrade, anxious now that he is alone, and stares uneasily into the darkness. Squinting suddenly, he believes he can see something floating before his eyes…"

"Is this a dagger I see before me," he asks himself, "its handle turned toward my hand?" He extends his hand to touch what he thinks is a pointed, shimmering knife, but it drifts quickly away and out of reach. "Come, let me clutch you!" He tries for the knife handle several more times. "I cannot grasp you, yet I can still see you – can't you be touched, fatal vision, the way you can be seen? …Or are you merely a dagger within my mind, something created by the fever in my blood? I still see you, as clear as the dagger which now I draw." He holds his knife up in the air to compare it with the one he imagines is there. "You guide me in the direction I was heading and are the very weapon I was planning to use!" He lowers his dagger, thinking he has pulled it from the air; he stares at the blade shining in the torchlight… "My eyes are playing tricks," he reasons, "or else they're all I can trust…"

Raising his eyes, he looks again. "I can still see you, and on your blade and handle are spots of blood that were not there a moment ago – " He lunges at the darkness in a panic, clutching madly at the imagined weapon, then just as quickly stops. "Nothing there," he realizes, glancing behind him at the torch, whose flame burns quietly away. "…Nothing there. – It's the bloody business we have at hand that makes me see this!" he pants to himself. "– Now, in blackest night when Nature seems dead to half the sleeping world and strange dreams torment the rest. – When covens of witches burn offerings to the demons of night, and the hooded reaper is wakened by the howls of his watchdog wolves, to creep, ghostly and silent, toward his victim. – You forces of earth and above, close your ears to my footsteps so their sound on these stones will not show you where I must go, or shake the dreadful silence, which so gravely suits this present deed."

Taking a breath, he collects himself, closes his eyes and opens them, a determined look spreading over his face. "While I rave, he goes on living. Words in the heat of action prompt worse fear and more misgiving!"

As he turns from the balustrade, a small bell rings lightly somewhere below.

Macbeth listens until silence resumes.

"I go, and it is done. The bell invites me! Pray you do not hear it, Duncan, for it is a knell that summons you to Heaven, or to Hell…"

He moves rapidly into the shadows, the torch in the archway burning quietly after he is gone….

Ten minutes have passed, the torch continuing to burn in the upper archway, when Lady Macbeth emerges from the darkness carrying a round tray on which she has a silver wine flagon and three pewter goblets, two that are turned upside down. Satisfied that no one is about, she sets the tray carefully on the balustrade, holds the flagon lid open with one hand while with the other she picks up the goblet that isn't turned over, and pours the last of the wine into it.

"What has made them drunk has made me bold," she boasts excitedly to herself, and drinks. "What doused their hot thirst has fanned the flames of my intent," she smiles then hurries to drink the rest of her wine. She finishes and takes a small medicine vial from the pocket of her dressing gown, a pleased look on her face – when a bird cries shrilly in the darkness.

"What's that?" she wonders nervously and spins around to see, bumping the wine tray with her leg so the goblets fall over and bang together. "Shh!" she scolds and quickly stands the three goblets upright, not breathing, while she remains motionless, listening.

The bird's screeching cry comes again. "The owl," she reminds herself, "crying cruel goodnight to those whose death is near…" She sighs, tense but relieved, her face brightening as it dawns on her: "He has done it by now. The doors will be open and the guards passed out on the floor, laughing in the face of duty with their coarse, drunken snores…"

She uncorks the small vial, leans over the baluster railing to empty it, but stops suddenly, reconsiders, and steps away from the light so as not to be seen pouring the contents out.

"Who's there?" Macbeth calls in a low voice from close by. "What is happening?" But in the darkness beyond the torchlight, Lady Macbeth doesn't hear.

" – No!" she says in a panic. "What if they have woken up and it has yet to happen! The attempt to kill a king, much as the act itself, could prove our complete undoing. Listen!" But all is dead silence. Her fingers toy with the medicine vial. "I laid out the daggers so he wouldn't miss them," she tells herself. " – I could have been the one to do it!" she declares, "if only Duncan hadn't looked exactly like my father did when sleeping – "

She breaks off because Macbeth has come forward into the light and approached the balustrade.

"Oh my husband!" Lady Macbeth cries joyfully and runs to embrace him, but halts when she sees his bare arms covered up to the elbows in Duncan's blood, a blood-coated dagger in each of his hands.

"I have done the deed," he says, as though he can't believe it. "Did you not hear a noise?"

She stares at the wet blood, mesmerized, and doesn't answer.

"Did you not hear a noise?" he asks again, more firmly.

"I heard the owl," she murmurs, distracted, "and I heard crickets – "

"When?"

"Just now."

"As I came down?"

"Yes."

"Listen!" he says, peering past her into the darkness, though everything is quiet. "Who was sleeping in the second room?"

Lady Macbeth lifts her eyes to meet his. "Donalbain."

Macbeth nods, letting the name register, and gives a frowning glance to the blood running down his arms, dripping from the knives. "This is a sorry sight…"

"Only a fool would say that – 'a sorry sight," she rebukes him.

"It must have been Donalbain," Macbeth continues to himself. "He laughed in his sleep, but then someone else cried 'Murder…' and in their noise they woke each other up. I stood there and listened, but they just said a short prayer and went back to sleep."

"The two sons were sleeping there," Lady Macbeth points out.

" ...One cried 'God bless', and the other answered 'Amen', as if they had seen me with this blood on me. Hearing their fear, I couldn't bring myself to say 'Amen' after they said 'God bless'."

"Don't think on it so much."

"But, why couldn't I say 'Amen'? I was most in need of blessing just then, yet 'Amen' stuck in my throat unsaid."

"We cannot think this way about what has happened or it will drive us mad."

"I could swear I heard a voice cry 'Sleep no more. Macbeth has murdered sleep.' Simple sleep: sleep that soothes our cares and woes, the end to each day's struggles. Easeful rest from work, the balm of troubled minds, great Nature's bounty, the nourishing essence of life's feast – "

"What does this mean?"

Macbeth ignores the question and carries on. " – And still the voice cried 'Sleep no more' to all the house. 'Glamis has murdered sleep, and therefore Cawdor shall sleep no more, Macbeth shall sleep no more!"

"Who was it that cried thus?" Lady Macbeth presses him, annoyed. "My God, worthy Thane, you weaken your noble self dwelling on such things. Fill a bucket at the well and wash the filthy evidence from your hands."

He holds up the daggers, looking puzzled.

"Why did you bring these with you?" Lady Macbeth says sharply. "They must be found there – put them in the sleeping sleeping guards' hands, and smear their clothes with blood as well. Go on."

"I'll not go back. I'm afraid to think of what it is I've done. I dare not see the sight again."

"Coward! Give me the daggers." She snatches them from him. "People who are dead or sleeping can do no harm – only a child believes that." She peers at him as though there's something else she wants to say, but decides not to. "If he's still bleeding, I'll coat the guards' hands and faces, for it has to look as if they killed him." She turns and hurries away.

Alone in the torchlight, Macbeth heaves a weary sigh and closes his eyes – but opens them, alarmed, when the sound of a heavy object pounding on the castle's great wooden door echoes through the dark, deserted courtyard.

Frenzied, he crosses to the balustrade and peers into the darkness below. "Where is that coming from? – What's happening to me when I jump at the slightest noise?" A desperate look on his face, he lowers his shaking head and leans forward to rest his hands on the railing, but realizing they will leave bloodstains, he stands up, clenching his fists in frustration. "Whose hands are these? Ha – they pluck out my eyes!" He turns his head away. "Would all the water in the ocean wash them of this blood? No, not now – these hands would turn the sea itself to blood, its green water running red…"

Holding out her blood-wet hands, Lady Macbeth suddenly rushes from the shadows. "Mine are now as red as yours." She lets him see. "But I would be ashamed if my heart were as white with fear – "

Avoiding her, Macbeth steps closer to the torch, just as the pounding at the castle door comes again.

"I hear knocking at the south gate," she says, frantic. "Let us go back to our chamber. A little water cleans us of the guilt. How easy it will be after that!" She stands between him and the torch. "Your courage has deserted you!"

The banging on the door continues.

"Still more knocking!" She takes his arm but he pulls it away. "Change into your dressing gown so that if we are called it won't seem as though were already up – " Still he refuses to move. "Don't lose yourself in weak thoughts!" she cries.

"Knowing what I have done, it would be better not to know myself…"

The knocking becomes so strident that, in a rage, Lady Macbeth reaches up and removes the torch from its mount. Unable to extinguish the flames by blowing on them, she begins smashing the torch against the wall until they are out, her panting breath the only sound in the total darkness…

"Wake Duncan with your knocking," Macbeth pleads, "if only you could…"

"Here's a racket indeed!" the porter of Glamis shouts as he emerges from his gatehouse to see who's so determined to enter the castle at this early hour. There is more than one person knocking on the great wooden door now. "If a man were tendin' the gates of Hell he'd have his hands as full as I," he complains, fumbling to do up his pants and shirt. His two helpers hobbling half-asleep from the gatehouse behind him, the porter shoos them toward the chain-wheel, has them fit the crank handle, undo the latches, slide the log bar out of its brackets.

"Knock, knock, knock!" he shouts, bothered and ornery. "Who's there in the name of Beelzebub?" He lends his helpers a hand with the work. "Here if it isn't the farmer who jacked his fees but hanged himself when the ruddy prices fell. Come right in and join the toil," he rails at whoever's knocking, "but just be sure you got plenty 'a rags to wipe your brow, cause you'll sweat it out in here."

The knocks resume once more, the porter shaking his head. "Knock, knock! Who's there in Satan's name? By God, maybe a double-dealer, playing all sides against the middle so's he can't say exactly where he stands any more. Come in, my double-dealing man!" He speaks again but his voice is drowned out by the urgent knocking.

"Knock, knock, knock! Who's there?" He and his helpers are almost ready to turn the crank. "God's name, it may be the thieving tailor who steals so much cloth the pants he makes fit tighter and tighter: come in, tailor! You can heat your iron in here, I tell you!"

As the knocking persists, the porter smirks at his helpers, enjoying the commotion he's causing. "Knock, knock! Not a moment's peace!" he carries on. "Who are you?" He clears his throat and spits a decent-sized gob at the door, waving his helpers to wait just a bit longer.

"Ah, this place is too cold to be Hell. I'll be the devil's sweat-boy no longer! Course I always thought I'd be letting in folks of the better persuasion," he yells so his sarcasm is sure to be heard, "the ones taking the easy route to the everlasting bonfire – "

Cut off by the relentless knocking, he signals for his men to start turning the chain-wheel at last. "Just a second, just a second!" Creaking on their huge hinges, the massive doors slowly swing open.

"Remember!" he yells his loudest, "a penny for the porter!"

The nobles Macduff and Lenox ride in and dismount.

"Up too late to be up so early, friend?" Macduff joshes the porter.

"By God, sir," he replies, "we were drinking till half past three. And drink, sir, gives rise to three things."

"What three things would they be then, sir?"

"By our Lady," the porter says with an air of authority, "it gives rise to red faces, sound sleep and much urine. As for pleasing the missus," he winks, "it gives rise, all right." He makes a fist and raises his arm. "But it gives way," he lets his arm go limp. "It gives rise to desire, but it ruins the performance. Therefore, much drinking plays tricks on a man in the mood, as they say. Why, it makes him, but it breaks him. It sharpens the blade, but dulls it too soon. Stands a man up straight, but gives him the slump. In the end, lust lies but in his dreams, and once he's lying, it leaves him lying…" He winks again at Macduff.

"As it left you lying last night," Macduff smirks, amused.

"That it did, sir," the porter nods, eyeing Macduff as he takes out his money pouch. "Drink had me by the throat. But I got back at him for throwing me down, and though he had me by the throat as I say, and took the legs out from under me, being stronger, I gave him what was coming to him."

"Is your master stirring?" Macduff asks, handing the porter some coins, but as he does so he notices Macbeth coming into the courtyard. "Well, our knocking has wakened him – here he is."

"Good day, noble Sir!" Lenox offers Macbeth a greeting hand.

"Good day to both of you."

"Is the King awake, worthy Thane?" Macduff asks.

"Not yet."

"He ordered me to appear first thing – I've almost missed the appointed hour."

"I'll take you to him," Macbeth says affably and walks his visitors across the courtyard and into the castle. Upstairs in the hall, just rising servants and household staff are busy beginning their day.

"I know this is welcome trouble for you, but it is trouble nonetheless," Macduff points out politely as they reach the end of a corridor and head through a door.

"Work that gives us pleasure is no discomfort," Macbeth assures him as they come outside and move along the upper archway. "This is the way," he says, stepping aside to let Macduff precede him through the door that leads into the King's quarters.

Macduff turns. "I'll go straight in myself for he'll be expecting me."

Macbeth remains behind with Lenox, who is gazing out at the first light of day.

"Is the King leaving here today?"

"Yes, he's planning to."

Coming away from the balustrade, Lenox catches sight of the burnt out torch and black char marks on the wall below the mount.

"Last night was a most unusual night." He replaces the torch in its mount and turns to regard Macbeth. "Where we were staying, the chimneys were all blown down, and people said they heard agonized cries in the wind, bone-chilling screams: omens of tumult and disruption, boding the advent of troubled times. – An owl screeched all night long. Some people said the earth shook and began, in some places, to quake."

"It was a rough night," Macbeth agrees.

"I can't remember one as bad in my short years."

But before Macbeth can comment further, Macduff returns from the King, a grave look on his face as he reels forward shouting: "Oh horror, horror, horror! No tongue can find words, no heart begin to grasp!"

"What's the matter?" Macbeth and Lenox ask at the same time.

"Destruction has created its masterpiece!" He looks at Macbeth, who remains unshaken. "Unholiest murder has broken into the Lord's sacred temple, my Thane, robbing the building of its life."

"What do you mean, 'its life'?"

"His Majesty?" Lenox asks, it dawning on him what Macduff might be saying.

"Go into his room and let your eyes be turned to stone by the ruinous sight. Don't ask me to speak of it – go and see for your selves," he orders them, stepping back to let them pass.

Taking deep breaths, Macduff comes across the archway to stand at the balustrade and get some air. "Wake up!" he shouts across the courtyard. "Wake up and sound the call to arms! Murder and treason!" he calls, "Banquo and Donalbain! Malcolm. All! Wake up! Shake off death's twin, drowsy sleep, and behold the thing itself," he points toward the King's room. "Get up, get up and glimpse the end of the world! Malcolm! Banquo! Rise like ghosts from your dead sleep and come witness this horror! Horror!"

A wool blanket wrapped around her, Lady Macbeth makes her way into the archway and confronts Macduff.

"For what awful reason does this noise summon the sleepers of this house from their beds? Tell me!"

"Oh, gentle lady, it would not be right for you to listen to the things I have to say. To repeat them in a woman's ear would kill her just to hear – "

Banquo is suddenly there.

"Banquo," Macduff mourns, "our royal master's murdered."

Shaken, Lady Macbeth can only stare. "No," she says, "it can't be…"

Macduff nods.

"No! Not in our house!"

"A terrible thing to happen anywhere," Banquo offers and casts his eyes at Macduff. "Contradict yourself and say it is not so, I beg you."

Just then, Macbeth and Lenox come out, looking grim.

"Had I but died an hour before this happened," Macbeth mourns, "I would have lived a blessed life. For from this moment on there's nothing to be valued in this world. All is but worthless and trifling. Honor and renown are dead. The wine of life has been poured. Nothing remains but the very dregs…"

Malcolm and his brother join the others.

"Is there some trouble?" Donalbain asks.

"More than you know," Macbeth tells him. "The spring from which your blood flows – the fountain and source – has been stopped."

"Your royal father has been murdered," Macduff says, mincing no words.

"That can't be! Murdered by whom?" Malcolm demands.

"His guards, or thus it appears," Lenox puts in. "Their hands and faces were stained with blood, as were their daggers. We found the weapons beside their pillows, not even wiped clean. They stared at us in bewildered frenzy, like they were no longer to be trusted."

" – I regret that in my fury I killed them," Macbeth adds.

"Why would you do that?" Macduff glares at him.

Macbeth looks into the faces of those around him as he speaks. "No one can be wise and astounded, calm and furious, loyal and neutral at the same time," passion mounting in his voice. "My instinct, my impetuous love for our King, overcame the dictates of reason. There lay Duncan, his silver-pale skin splashed with royal blood, and the stab wounds struck the eye like gaping holes through which death had ripped its way into his body. And there were the murderers, still wet with the bloody evidence of their attack, their daggers smeared with raw, red gore – what loving heart could have held back and not had the courage to make that love known?"

"Help me away from here – " Lady Macbeth cries and starts to faint, Banquo lunging to catch her.

"Look to the Lady," Macduff calls, watching Macbeth.

While Lady Macbeth is tended to, Malcolm takes Donalbain aside. "Why are we keeping silent when this business affects us most of all?"

"What can we say while we remain here, where our fate waits in ambush, perhaps to attack us also. Let us be gone. Our tears are not yet ready."

"Nor our deep sorrow to be truly felt."

"Look to the Lady," Banquo says to the servants carrying the unconscious Lady Macbeth inside. " – And once we are dressed against this shivering cold, let us meet and look further into this bloody deed to know what happened. Fears and doubts shake us in their own way: I put myself in God's great hands, and with His help I will fight against those whose foul purpose was behind this treacherous act of evil."

"As will I," says Macduff.

"And so will we all," the others agree.

"Let's arm ourselves and gather in the hall," Macbeth suggests.

Banquo, Macduff and the other nobles in accord, they quickly disperse, leaving Malcolm and Donalbain alone outside the room where the body of their dead father lies.

"What will you do?" Malcolm asks his brother. "I'm not for joining them. It's easy for a traitor in their midst to wear the guise of sorrow which he doesn't truly feel. I will go to England."

"I, to Ireland. We will be safer if we separate. Here, smiling men may be ready with their daggers – those who are closest to us now have greater reason to shed this blood of ours."

Nodding, Malcolm's face is somber. "This murderous course is far from finished. To be safe we must stay beyond striking distance. Therefore let us not stand on ceremony but take to our horses and fly. There's reason enough to steal away, if staying here we are to die…"

Storm clouds are scudding across the dark sky when the noble Rosse and his band of men come riding toward a narrow wooden bridge that is packed to the railings with sheep, an old man herding the animals forward and off to the side of the road. Catching sight of the approaching horsemen, the old man lets his flock graze on roadside grass while he lingers by the bridge, waving the curved end of his shepherd's crook at Rosse, who signals his men to stop. For a moment the only sound is the rush of water passing under the bridge.

"In all my seventy years," the old man declares, "I've seen my share of strange and dreadful things, but they're nothing compared with this storm we had last night."

"Well, my good old man," Rosse replies, "when the heavens threaten the earth like that, it's usually because of the bloody deeds performed by men." He raises his eyes and gives the sky a glance. "According to the clock it's day, but dark night still blocks the sun. Is it the night's strength or the day's shame that darkness entombs the earth like this when it should be radiant with living light?"

"It's unnatural," the old man warns, resting both hands on his crook and shaking his head, "even as the cruel deed was against the

King. Tuesday last a falcon soaring freely was attacked and killed by an owl hunting mice."

Rosse nods. "And, believe it or not, Duncan's horses, handsome and swift – the best of their breed – turned wild and fierce, broke out of their stalls and fled into the fields, rearing up as if bucking invisible riders. They charged anyone who came near, as if they were at war with mankind."

"I was told they ate each other."

"Yes, and I watched in amazement as they did so," Rosse says grimly, one of his men giving word that someone is coming up behind. Rosse turns in his saddle.

"The good Macduff. How goes the world of late?" he asks lightly.

"You haven't heard?"

"Is it known in fact who did this worse than bloody deed?"

"The men Macbeth killed, it seems."

"A sad day," Rosse shakes his head. "What could they have hoped to gain?"

"It's sure they were acting on bribes. Yet Malcolm and Donalbain have fled, which now puts the cloud of suspicion on them to have done it."

"Things ever more unnatural," Rosse smiles ruefully at the old man. "Devouring ambition bites off the hand that feeds it." He turns back to Macduff. "So Macbeth will become king?"

"He has already been named and gone to Scone for his coronation."

"Where is Duncan's body?"

"He was taken to Colmekill, the sacred tomb where his ancestors are buried."

"Will you attend at Scone?"

Macduff shakes his head. "No, cousin, I'm heading home to Fife."

"Well, I shall go for the coronation."

"May you see only good things done there," Macduff says, sarcasm evident in his voice. "So, adieu." He grips Rosse's hand in farewell. "In case old loyalties give way in face of those that are new!" He stares at Rosse to let what he has said sink in, then turns and spurs his horse toward the bridge, hooves of his followers' horses thundering on the ancient wood structure behind him.

"Farewell," Rosse says to the old man.

"God's blessing go with you," the old man smiles gently, "and with those who would make good out of bad, friends out of foes…"

3.1

A blustery afternoon wind has the flags of Scotland, Cawdor and Glamis flapping high atop the royal palace at Forres. Sentries are posted along the castle's upper ramparts and at the gates below, keeping a close eye on Duncan's servants and household staff who are quietly vacating the castle: glum-looking men and women carrying their meager possessions in their arms or on their backs, those riding in the rickety wagons and baggage carts gazing forlornly back at the place they have called home for so many years…

Meanwhile, the mood inside the castle throne room, festooned with colorful flags, banners and coats-of-arms representing the new hierarchy and its royal affiliations, is one of jubilant celebration, Macbeth, now King, and Lady Macbeth, his Queen, basking in the congratulations and good wishes of their noble friends and allies.

Making his way forward in the line to be received by the new monarch and his wife, Banquo watches as Macbeth shares an amusing anecdote with several knights, Lady Macbeth smiling politely beside him, her added comments prompting a jovial response from both the knights.

"You have it all now," Banquo says of Macbeth, "King, Cawdor, Glamis, just as the weird sisters promised, though I fear you've done some great evil to make it yours. Yet it was also said that kingship would not outlive you, that I myself would be the father of many kings. As now their words reflect the truth they told, Macbeth, might it not be that what the sisters said could come to pass for me as well, and see my greatest hopes fulfilled? But hush, no more – "

"Here's our most important guest," Macbeth greets Banquo as he steps forward to be received.

"If he had been forgotten," Lady Macbeth chimes in, "his absence from our great feast would have been most unbecoming."

"Tonight we hold our coronation dinner, sir, and I would most enjoy your presence at our table."

"My foremost duty is ever to obey what you command, your Highness," he bows.

Macbeth accepts the gesture with a grateful smile and turns his friend away from the crowd for a word in private. "Tell me, are you going riding this afternoon?"

"Yes, my good lord."

"If you weren't, we would have valued your advice in this afternoon's council meeting. It is always most wise and helpful – but we'll hear it tomorrow. Will you be riding far?"

"As far as I can between now and supper, my lord. Unless my horse is faster than I think, it might be an hour or two after dark before I return."

"Don't miss our feast," Macbeth reminds him with a playful nudge on the shoulder.

"There is not a chance I would, my lord."

"We hear that our murderous cousins are living in England and Ireland," Macbeth says pointedly, "though they have yet to admit killing their father. Word has come that they are spreading vicious lies about us." Banquo nods in acknowledgement of the news.

"But again, we will talk of this tomorrow, when state matters bring us together. Get to your horse now, and farewell until tonight. Is Fleance going along?" Macbeth asks as an afterthought.

"Yes, my lord – and we should indeed be on our way."

"May your horses carry you swiftly and safely," he says, and surprises Banquo by embracing him. "I trust them to look after you," he adds. "Farewell…"

Moving back to the throne, Macbeth waits while conversation stops and the room falls silent.

"Every one should do as he likes until seven this night. To appreciate your company all the more, we will keep to ourselves until suppertime. In the meantime, God be with you!"

"God be with you!" the crowd responds, and begins to disperse following the departure of Lady Macbeth and her entourage. Retreating to a corner of the room behind the throne, Macbeth motions to one of his servants.

"Have the men I sent for arrived?"

"They are waiting outside the gate, my Lord."

Macbeth opens a door built to look like part of the wall. "Bring them here," he says and slips inside.

Though there is a small window, the candle-lit chamber is more a vault than a room, filled with historical relics, artifacts and treasure, from suits of armor, shields and swords, to scrolls, chalices and fine cloth. Macbeth comes in and gazes idly about the room, lifting the lid of a small wooden chest to see what's inside.

"To be king is nothing unless I am safely so: my fear of Banquo runs deep, the regal virtues which rule his nature more than just unsettling. He is brave and bold, and with that fearless spirit he has a wisdom that keeps his courage from reckless action. There is no one I fear more than he. In his presence my confidence diminishes, as it is said Mark Anthony's did alongside mighty Caesar." In the jewel chest he finds several rings, picks one studded with a red ruby and slips it on his finger. "Banquo went boldly at the Weird Sisters when they hailed me as Cawdor and King, demanding that they also speak to him, which they promptly did, with their prophecy that he would be the source of a line of kings. On my head they have placed a fruitless crown," he rails in frustration, "and in my hand a pointless scepter – to be seized by one not of my blood, since no son of mine, the Sisters say, will ever mount the throne. If this is to be so, then it's for Banquo's children that I have gone and corrupted myself, for them that I murdered the gracious Duncan, for them poisoned my own peace of mind." He bows and shakes his head ruefully, staring at the ruby ring. "I have handed my eternal soul, a man's immortal jewel, to the devil himself in order to make them kings – the children of Banquo, kings!"

He removes the ring, replaces it in the chest and slams the lid closed. "Never. Come Fate, I dare you to fight me!" A knock comes at the door. "To the death," he finishes. "Who's there?"

The servant enters with two men in hooded cloaks.

"Wait outside until we're done," Macbeth tells him. "Wasn't it yesterday we spoke together?" he asks, motioning for the men to remove their hoods.

"It was, your Highness," the first man answers.

"Well then, have you thought over what we talked about?" Both men nod. "You know that it was Banquo who deprived you of your land and livelihood, not I?" Again the men nod. "Though you blamed me for your trouble. But as long as this was made clear to you in our previous conversation…I believe I gave you proof enough as to how you were deceived and defeated – by whom, how it was done and why, which shows beyond all doubt that it was Banquo's doing, which even a halfwit or a madman would agree upon without persuading."

"You made this known to us," the first man acknowledges sullenly.

"Indeed. And ventured further, which is the purpose of this our second meeting. Do you find your patience such that you can let this go? Are you so devout that you would pray for this good man – and for his children – whose heavy hand has burdened you till you die, and made your families beggars forever?"

"We are men, my lord," the first man says defiantly.

"Yes, in the scheme of things you might pass for men, in the same way wolfhounds, greyhounds, terriers and spaniels are called 'dogs.' But the qualities of a breed are what distinguish it from others as swift or slow, as fierce or friendly, as house-dogs or hunters – each according to the gifts generous nature has provided, whereby each kind stands out in the list that has them down as simply 'dogs.' It's the same with men. Now, if you are better than the rank and file of humanity, say so, and I will put to you a proposal which, if it's carried out, will vanquish your enemy and endear you to me in lasting friendship." He meets their eyes with an icy stare. "As long as Banquo lives, I suffer the sickness his death alone will cure."

"I am someone, my Lord," the second man speaks up, "who is so enraged by the battering the world has given me, that I am desperate for a chance to get back at those who have mistreated me."

"And I am the same," the first man sneers, "so weary of disasters, of being knocked about by fortune, that I would risk anything to better my life, or let it be ended."

"You both know Banquo was your enemy."

"We do, my Lord," the second man offers.

"He is mine as well: such a threat to me that every minute he remains alive is like a knife thrusting at my very heart. Though with the power I wield I could simply destroy him and justify his death as the will of the King, I must not do so. He and I have friends between us whose loyalty I cannot do without, so I must appear to mourn his death as others will, even the death I myself will cause. Thus it is I ask your help to keep this business secret, for various important reasons."

"We shall perform whatever you command, my Lord."

"Even if it means our lives – "

"Your courage is not in doubt," Macbeth assures them. "Within an hour at most I will tell you where to wait for him who knows the place and time it should be done, for it must be done tonight and at some distance from the castle. Remember well that I must be kept clear of any blame, and that the job must be completed without error or mistake. Fleance, who will be with him, is equally a threat, and so must share the same fate as his father in that dark hour." He walks them to the door. "Go and make your minds up – I'll be with you shortly."

"Our minds are made up, my Lord," the second man declares as he raises the hood of his cloak.

"We are ready, my Lord," the first man agrees.

Macbeth looks each man in the eye. "I'll send for you. Stay close by."

While they leave, he gazes toward the window, his own mind made up now. "It is settled; Banquo, if to heaven your soul will take flight, it will make the journey there tonight."

Lady Macbeth is restless and pacing fretfully in her chamber when she stops by the window and sits down at her table, littered with letters she has written but crumpled up. She takes a quill pen, dips it fast into the ink pot, and scratches furiously on a fresh piece of paper as if there is something she wants to put down before she forgets. The nib bends in half, soft from too much black ink. Annoyed, she stands, goes to the door and calls for a servant. In a moment one enters, after knocking, and bows to Lady Macbeth. She shows him the broken pen and asks for some fresh quills. Giving a respectful nod, he heads for the door.

"Has Banquo left the castle?" Lady Macbeth calls across the room.

"Yes, madam," the servant says, "but he will return tonight."

Lady Macbeth nods. "Would the King – " she begins, but pauses. " – Tell the King I would like to speak with him."

"Madam, I will." He turns briskly and leaves.

Lady Macbeth continues moving about, her eyes roaming the large, regal bedroom, although she appears absorbed in thought as she was moments earlier.

"Nothing is gained," she muses to herself, "all happiness is lost, when we get what we desire, but question the cost." She sits on the edge of her bed, thinking. "Is it better perhaps to be what we destroy, than by our destruction live in doubtful joy?"

Just as she's speaking, the door opens and Macbeth comes into the room, looking about to see who she's talking to. She gets up from the bed, rushes and embraces him.

"How are you, my Lord?" she asks into his chest, Macbeth glancing over at the paper-and-ink mess on her writing table rather than returning the embrace. "Why do you keep to yourself," she continues, "with anxious worry your only companion? Dwelling on thoughts that should have died when he you are fixed on thinking about, did? It does no good to brood about things that cannot be helped – what's done is done."

"We have but wounded the snake, not killed it," Macbeth despairs. "It will heal and regain its strength, and our worst fears will once again be vulnerable to its fangs. I would rather see the universe collapse, heaven and earth destroyed, than be wracked with worry in every waking moment, and suffer, too, the terrible dreams that torment our nightly sleep. We would be better off with the dead whom we, to gain our peace, have sent to their peace, than continue to live with our minds in anxious frenzy. Duncan is in his grave. He sleeps well now that his life's troubles are over. Treason has done its worst. Poisoned friendship, civil war, foreign invasions: nothing can touch him now…"

"Come, my noble Lord," Lady Macbeth responds, smiling as she steps back and regards his face. "Smooth over your frowns. Be bright and lively among your guests tonight."

Macbeth lifts her arms away. "So I shall, my Love, and so should you. Remember to pay great attention to Banquo. Show him high respect in your words and actions: we're still not safe, so we must wash away any hint of dishonor in streams of flattery, making masks of our faces, thereby disguising that which is truly within our hearts."

"You must stop this brooding," she pleads.

"Oh dear wife, my mind is full of scorpions! You know that Banquo and Fleance live."

"But they're not made to live forever."

"There's comfort in that. They can be dealt with. Thus be jovial and merry. Before the bat has flown from its hiding place, before Hecate, goddess of evil, calls forth the June beetle to lull the night with its drowsy hum, a dreadful deed will at last be done."

"Dreadful deed?"

"You're better off not knowing, dearest, till you can applaud the deed." He moves to the window and gazes out. "Come, concealing Night," he says, in a voice somber with invocation, "blindfold the tender eye of Pitying Day, and with your bloody and invisible hand cancel and tear in pieces longtime bonds of friendship." His voice shakes. Stepping closer to the window, he peers out. "The light is growing dim. The crow flies toward the darkening forest. The good things of Day are drifting toward sleep, while Night's black forces awaken to hunt their prey." He turns to his wife. "My words amaze you," he remarks. "But keep yourself calm. Once begun, bad things by their evil grow strong. So, let us be on our way." He moves toward the door and waits for her to follow.

She takes several steps, but hesitates. Looking into his face, she doesn't appear to know why….

Evening is starting to fall in the forest as three men in hooded cloaks tether their horses by the light of a torch one man is holding. They head through the trees, twigs snapping underfoot as they hurry forward, the man with the torch grumbling in a surly voice: "But who told you to join us?"

"Macbeth," the third man replies.

"We can trust him," the second man says. "Remember, the man gave us our instructions."

"Stay with us then," the first man grunts as they reach the edge of the forest and peer through the trees at an open area where two roads come together. The three men huddle by the light of the torch, the first man holding it up for a look at the third man's face, but he turns away, which prompts another peevish grunt from the first man as he glances toward the sky. "There's streaks of light still glimmering in the west," he remarks to the second man. "This time of day, those on the road move swiftly to reach the inn before darkness sets in. The ones we're waiting for should be here soon," he says, lowering the torch.

" – Listen! I hear horses," the third man says, glancing behind him the next moment to see the first man grinding the torch into the ground to put it out. Over the man's protests, he snatches it away while it's still burning and steps into the road, holding it up high.

"Give us a light there!" Banquo calls.

"The light, the light!" the second man worries, but the third man is already approaching Banquo. "It's him!" he calls back to the others.

"Get ready!" the first man whispers and moves onto the road.

Banquo slows his horse, Fleance riding up behind. "It looks like rain tonight," Banquo says, thinking the third man is coming forward to greet him, but instead he shoves the torch in Banquo's face so he can't see.

"Then let it pour!" the first man shouts, taking his torch and hurling it at Banquo, while the second man rushes from the other side and pulls Banquo off his horse.

"Traitors!" Banquo yells as he goes down. "Run, Fleance, run!" Leaping to his feet the moment he lands, Banquo reaches for his sword but the second man and the third man are thrusting their swords repeatedly. "Run!" Banquo shouts helplessly to his son. "Run! Live to have vengeance! Oh...worthless – " Fatally hurt, he slumps to the ground, blood gurgling from his mouth with his final moan.

"You threw away the light!" the third man explodes.

"That was the thing to do," the first man snarls in his own defense, returning to stand with the others.

"The one was killed, but the son escaped."

"The job was only half done," the second man says uneasily.

"Well, we will go and report what happened – " the first man says, but his next words are cut off as the third man, torch in hand, crashes from the forest on his horse and charges off down the road at full gallop.

The first man grabs Banquo's feet and starts dragging the body toward the forest. He asks for help, but the second man has his eyes on the torch flame, quickly growing smaller in the distance, until finally its light disappears altogether...

With rows of flaming torches lining the walls, candles aplenty burning on the long oak tables, and a fire of trunk-sized logs blazing in the hearth, a banquet is about to commence in the Great Hall of Forres Castle, the assembled nobles, knights and royal followers rising from their seats as Macbeth and Lady Macbeth, accompanied by Rosse, Lenox, and the highest Lords of the Realm, move through the hushed silence to the front of the room.

"You know your ranks," Macbeth's voice rings out as the procession gathers at the head table, "so take your places accordingly." There follows some shuffling, jovial chatter and changing of places. When all are ready, Macbeth takes up a silver wine goblet. "To my subjects high and low: I bid you welcome."

Lords and nobles around the room raise their wine goblets in response.

"Thanks to your Majesty!" they reply, their boisterous voices together in unison.

"We will mingle with each of you in turn as befits a humble host, while our hostess will keep her seat for now but welcome you in due course."

"Give greetings, sir, to all our friends," Lady Macbeth smiles from her seat, "for indeed they are heartily welcome."

The guests lift their goblets once more in a hearty toast: "Thanks to the Queen!"

Stewards, servants and household staff stream into the hall with the first of the food, taking up their appointed positions and waiting until the head table is ready before they serve the royal feast

As people take their seats around him, a smiling Macbeth leans toward his wife, "See how they greeted you with whole-hearted thanks?" Lady Macbeth nods, pleased, but directs her husband's eyes to the guests who are waiting to be seated. "There are equal numbers on both sides," he determines with a glance along the length of the table. "I shall sit here in the middle." He moves to take his place, but just as he's sitting down he notices a steward on the far side of the room motioning discreetly for his attention: the first of Banquo's murderers has come in and is intent on talking with the King.

His wine goblet still in hand, Macbeth promptly excuses himself and steps back from the table. "Enjoy yourselves freely," he urges his guests. "Once underway, we'll pass a goblet round the table in celebration…" he promises, his voice trailing off as he turns abruptly to leave, his going saved from being awkward by the bustling arrival of the servants with their enormous platters of food…

On his way across the room, Macbeth is forced to clink goblets and toast with several well-wishing followers who hold their tankards out to him as he passes. By the time he reaches the first man, the steward has ushered him to a corner, where neither of the men can be seen by guests at the banquet.

"There's blood on your face," Macbeth speaks first.

"It's Banquo's then."

"Better it be there than flowing in his veins. Is he dead?"

"My Lord, his throat is cut. I saw to it myself."

"You are the best of the cut-throats then," Macbeth says, pleased with the news.

"Yet he's just as good who did the same to Fleance. If that was you as well, you are without equal."

The first man clears his throat uncomfortably. "Most royal Sir," he explains, "Fleance escaped."

Macbeth stares at the man in disbelief. "Escaped?"

The first man nods.

"Then I am still plagued," Macbeth declares. " – I wanted to be sure, my position solid, rock hard, free as the surrounding air!" he rails. "But now I'm caged, confined, closed in – a prisoner to deepening doubts and fears. But Banquo's looked after?"

"Yes, my good Lord. He lies safe in the forest, wounded in twenty places, the least of them fatal."

"Thanks for that. The grown serpent out of the way," he reasons, "though not the young one, who could easily be the more poisonous – but he is without fangs for now.

"Leave me to my guests. We'll talk again tomorrow."

When the steward has escorted the first man from the room, Macbeth makes his way back to the head table, Lady Macbeth catching his eye as he returns.

"My royal Lord," she scolds, "you're not playing the cordial host. The guests might as well be visiting an inn if you don't assure them of their welcome during the meal. They would be better off dining at home if they're simply eating – good company and attention to courtesies are what make for a pleasant occasion. Otherwise, it's simply people gathered around a table."

"Thanks, I stand well reminded, dearest." Turning to his noble guests, he holds up his wine goblet. "May good digestion accompany hearty appetite – and good health to both!"

"Would your Highness grace us with His royal company?" Lenox asks, indicating Macbeth's seat toward the middle of the table.

Macbeth acknowledges Lenox and heads toward the chair. "We would have the nobility of the entire country under one roof," he allows, "if only Banquo were here to grace us with his presence. I hope I will have to fault him for a show of bad manners rather than pity him because it's some misfortune which keeps him away."

As he finishes speaking and is about to sit down, Banquo suddenly appears and slips into the seat ahead of him.

"His absence is rude, Sir," Rosse agrees, "since he promised he would be back on time." He repeats the invitation: "Would your Highness be good enough to honor us with your royal company?"

But Macbeth can only stare in horror at Banquo: his pale, bruised face, his blood-soaked clothes, torn in all the places where he's been stabbed.

" – The table's full!" Macbeth exclaims.

"Sir, we've saved the seat for you," Lenox laughs.

"Where?" Macbeth demands, confused.

"Here, my good Lord," Lenox says, touching the back of Macbeth's empty chair. "What is it that has upset your Highness?"

"Which of you has done this to me?" Macbeth demands of those at the table.

Rosse, Lenox and the other nobles exchange puzzled looks. "Done what, my Lord?" several of them ask.

"You cannot say I did it!" Macbeth shrieks at the ghost of Banquo, who turns his head slowly from side to side. "Don't shake your blood-soaked hair at me!"

"Gentlemen, rise," a concerned Lord Rosse instructs the table, "his Majesty is not well."

Lady Macbeth is quickly on her feet and attempting to smooth things over. "Sit, worthy friends. My Lord is often this way and has been from his youth," she explains. "Please, keep your seats. This will pass and he will be recovered in no time at all – if you pay it too much attention it will only upset him and the outburst could prolong itself."

She takes her husband by the arm and leads him away from the table, Macbeth staring back at the empty chair. "Eat," she urges the guests in a calm voice. "Pay him no mind."

Far enough from the table that none of the others can hear, she looks him sternly in the eye. "Are you a man?"

"Yes," he shoots back stubbornly, "and a brave one who is not afraid to look at something that would frighten the devil if – "

"Nonsense!" she rebukes him under her breath. "Your fear is making you see things that aren't really there: like the floating dagger you said was what led you to Duncan. These fits of fear that come over you," she frowns in frustration, "there's no reason for them at all –

there's nothing in the world to be afraid of. Shame on you! Why do you make such faces?" She reaches out her hand, takes him by the chin and turns his face toward hers. "You're staring at a chair – " she says slowly.

"Look, do you see that!" he cries, pointing toward Banquo still sitting at the table. "Go ahead, look!" he says, and points at his chair. "See? What do you say to that?" he demands. When she reacts by shaking her head, he breaks away, stalks toward the table and glares violently at the empty chair. "What do I care?" he demands of Lenox, Rosse and the others, who are looking on in utter amazement. "If you can nod," he shrieks at Banquo, "why can't you speak?" He steps closer until he is right beside the chair. " – If our tombs and graves are sending back the dead and buried, we might as well leave them for the vultures to eat – let *their* stomachs be crypts for the deceased!" He draws his sword and swings it – but the blade passes right through Banquo's ghostly neck and, rising from the chair, he glides easily toward the fire in the hearth, Macbeth rushing at him from behind and thrusting his sword for all he's worth, Banquo glancing back over his shoulder as he vanishes in the leaping flames…

A forced smile for her bewildered guests, Lady Macbeth waves them to sit down as she makes her way over to Macbeth, who continues staring at the fire, a forlorn look on his face. She turns him around so his back is to the guests. "Has foolishness completely stripped you of your manhood?"

"As sure as I stand here, he was in my seat," Macbeth answers meekly.

"Oh, for shame!"

Macbeth stares at his sword, where the blade went through Banquo's neck. "Blood has been shed before now," he broods, "in olden days, before laws came into place that were to end violence. Yet even so, murders too terrible for words have been committed: indeed, there was a time when a man beaten senseless would be left by the road for dead and that was the end of it. But now the dead rise again – wounds that killed them bleeding still – and sit down at our table. This is more strange than ever murder could be."

Lady Macbeth thinks quickly. "My worthy Lord," she says as

though nothing untoward has happened, "your noble friends miss you." She glances at Macbeth, motions with her eyes toward the table, where people have gradually resumed eating.

"I had forgotten," he admits. "Don't worry, my most worthy friends!" And he moves back to his place at the table. "I have an unusual malady, which is no concern to those who know me." He smiles appreciatively at Lady Macbeth. "Come, love and health to all!" he says keenly. I'll take my seat." He sits. "Give me some wine," he calls to the closest servant, who steps forward with a flagon and begins pouring into Macbeth's goblet. "Fill it full. I drink to the general joy of the whole table, and to our dear friend Banquo, who is absent from among us. If only he were here!" He hoists his goblet. "To one and all we drink," he toasts, "and to him! Good health!"

"Good health and our duty to you!" the nobles respond with their goblets raised.

" – Begone!" Macbeth hollers suddenly, shoots to his feet and in a fury, flings his silver goblet at the fireplace where Banquo has reappeared. "Out of my sight and let the earth hide you!" he rages. "Your bones have no marrow! Your blood is cold! There is no sight in those glaring eyes of yours!"

"Good Lords," Lady Macbeth hastens to explain, "think of it as a habit he can't help, nothing more." She fixes Macbeth with a cold glare. "Only it is spoiling the pleasure of the evening," she says pointedly.

"What any man dares, I dare as well," Macbeth boasts. "Come at me like a rabid Russian bear, charge like the horned rhinoceros, the Indian tiger! – Take any shape other than yourself, and my steady nerve will not falter. Or come back to life altogether and dare me to contest you man against man in some desolate place. If I tremble then, call me coward." He draws his sword and advances on the logs blazing in the hearth. "Leave this place, horrible shadow! Unreal mockery! Away with you!"

But by the time the words have left his mouth, Banquo's ghost has disappeared.

"Why, so…" he mutters, the logs in the fire crackling before his eyes. A peaceful look comes into his perspiring face. He sheathes his sword. "Now that it has gone," he informs the others quietly, "I am a man again. – Please, stay seated…"

"You've ruined the enjoyment of all," Lady Macbeth bristles, approaching him beside the fireplace. "Broken up our banquet feast over this passing strange 'sight'."

Macbeth gazes at the red wine splashed on the stone fireplace, his silver goblet lying on the floor below. "Can such things happen? Come over us suddenly as in a dream and not have us wonder what we have become?" He searches Lady Macbeth's face. "You make me feel I do not know myself: when you can regard sights like this and not lose the natural flush in your face, while mine turns full white and pale with fear…"

"What sights are these, my Lord?" Rosse inquires.

Macbeth looks over at the table, unsure of what he's being asked.

"Don't speak to him just yet," Lady Macbeth says, "he grows worse the more you talk." She takes her husband by the arm, but instead of returning him to the table she heads to the side of the room where he talked with the first murderer. "Good night to you all," she says over her shoulder. "Don't stand on ceremony, but depart quickly."

"Good night," Lenox calls to her, "and may his Majesty be returned to health!"

"A fond good night to you all," she says in farewell and carries on across the room as the guests make haste to the doors of the great hall.

"It will have blood, they say," Macbeth murmurs. "Blood will have blood. Stones have been known to move. Trees have tried to speak. Magpies, blackbirds, even the crows have sounded prophecies with their cries, telling who the murderer is." He lets out a breath and gazes around the empty banquet hall, plates that people walked away from a moment ago still laden with food, torches and candles blazing in every corner of the room, the great log fire burning away. "What time is it?" he asks his wife.

"Half way between night and morning. It's hard to tell."

After a moment, Macbeth meets her eyes: distant and unhappy. "What do you think of Macduff refusing our command to be present here tonight?"

"Have you sent for him?"

He shakes his head. "I heard, from some talking of it, that he would not come. I will send for him now." He gazes over at the table where the highest lords and nobles were seated. "In every one of their homes I have a servant who is paid to spy. Tomorrow – and I shall see that it is early – I will go to the Weird Sisters and have them tell me more, for now I am bent on knowing the worst that may befall me, through their worst means if I have to. I must devote myself to doing what is best for me, above every consideration." He shakes his head sadly. "I am so steeped in blood that going back is as wearisome a thought as carrying on. I have strange visions in my head which I know I must act upon, things I must attend to before I think of them too much."

"A restful sleep will help you feel better," says Lady Macbeth, talking to herself as much as to him.

"Come then," Macbeth says, "we'll get some sleep." He puts an arm around her shoulder as they walk slowly through the deserted hall. "My strangeness toward this illusion," he says idly, "was but the fear that passes with practice. And I am only just beginning…"

The rock cairn a smooth, crescent-shaped mound under the light of the full moon, the three witches are lying on their backs looking up at the stars as a dark-cloaked figure stands over them.

"Why, Hecate, you look *angry*," the first witch says.

"*Angerly*," her bearded twin sister repeats playfully.

The third witch, whose face is nose-less but has nostrils, begins hooting wildly until a snowy owl flies out from under Hecate's cloak and into the witch's mouth, to shut her up.

"Have I not reason, hags that you are, so brazen and bold that you would dare, to trade and traffic with Macbeth, in riddles and affairs of death? While I the goddess of all charms, mean contriver of all harms, was never asked to play my part, and show the glory of our art? And what is worse, all you have done has been but for a willful son: spiteful and angry, who as others do, loves for his own ends, not for you."

"Now is the time to make amends, so get below, and in the morning I will all my magic show, when this Macbeth comes here to know, where Destiny will have him go. Your cauldrons and your spells provide, your charms and everything beside. I am off into the air – wreaking havoc everywhere. Great things will happen very soon – before the human clock says noon!"

She points up to the sky. "Look, sisters, upon the cusp of yonder moon, a bright orb hangs with celestial power. I'll make it mine within the hour, pluck the orb and with my skill, conjure sprites to do my will, that by the strength of their illusion, Macbeth will suffer in confusion. Spurning fate, scorning death, hopes without wisdom, virtue or fear: Macbeth knows not what we know all, that pride goes always before a fall."

The third witch coughs and the snowy owl flies out of her mouth and over to Hecate, where in the blink of an eye, it becomes a little girl in white.

"Hark! My little spirit, see? Tomorrow she will lead Macbeth to me."

"Come away," the girl says and holds out her hand for Hecate to take.

"I am called," Hecate says, and suddenly she is gone.

The first witch gets up and turns to the others. "Come, let's hurry, enough of the moon. Knowing Hecate, she'll be back again soon…"

Just after dawn, the gates of Forres swing closed as Lord Lenox rides away from the castle at a gallop. On the road until the castle is no longer in sight, he veers off and heads into the countryside across fields white with snow that has fallen during the night. Riding hard for several miles, he slows approaching a forest grove, finds a path through the trees, and soon reaches a clearing where another horse and rider are waiting.

Dismounting, Lenox greets his fellow Lord and, with the only sound their horses' breath steaming in the frosty air, the two men talk.

"What I've been saying is now borne out by what I know is on your mind," Lenox begins. "You can figure for yourself the rest. I'll only add that strange things have been happening more and more. 'The gracious Duncan was pitied by Macbeth,'" he says with scoffing sarcasm. " – That may be, but after the King was dead. 'And most valiant Banquo was out riding in the dark.'" Lenox makes a face. "You can say, if you like, that Fleance killed him because Fleance ran away, but a man who rides after dark should lose his life?" Lenox is livid. "Who can't help but think how horrible it must have been for Malcolm and Donalbain to kill their gracious father?" he continues. "A dreadful deed, and Macbeth grieved over it, did he not? Did he not in a fit of holy rage as well, go in and kill the 'criminals' who were merely drunk and half-asleep? Wasn't that a noble deed?" he rants. "Yes, and a wise one too, 'for wouldn't it have angered anyone with feeling in his heart to hear the men deny the deed?'" He kicks a foot in frustration. "This is why I say he has managed things well. And I think if he had Duncan's sons under lock and key – which I hope to heaven he never will – he would teach them what happens when you kill a father. And Fleance too. But enough," Lenox says, his bitter point made. "I hear Macduff is in disgrace because he has spoken his mind, and because he failed to attend the tyrant's feast. Do we know where he has gone?"

"Duncan's son, whose birthright this tyrant has stolen, lives at court in England. The most holy King Edward has welcomed him with such respect that Malcolm's fall from fortune has not diminished by a jot the generous treatment he receives. Macduff is headed there to beseech the holy King to aid Malcolm by rousing the people in the border lands under their hero Siward. With their help – and God on their side – we may once more have food on our tables, peaceful sleep at night, feasts and banquets free from bloodshed, loyalty to our leader, and honor from our followers – all of which we long for now. And news of this has so angered Macbeth he is preparing against attack."

"Did he send you to summon Macduff?"

"He did, and with a firm 'Not I' the haughty messenger turned his back on me and scowled as if to say 'You will regret the day you gave that as your answer.'"

"That should warn Macduff to caution – to keep his distance

more than ever from Macbeth." He gets on his horse and waits while the Lord mounts his. "If only some holy angel could fly to the court of England and deliver Macduff's message before he gets there, so that blessed good fortune might soon return to this our grieving land, suffering now under Macbeth's cursèd hand."

"I'll say my prayers for that," the Lord replies.

A farewell shake of hands and the two men ride off through the woods, the first flakes of fresh snow beginning to fall...

Lenox waits on his horse while Macbeth dismounts and approaches the circular rock cairn, running his eyes over the massive gray stones which look to have been formed into this drab, crescent-shaped monument during ancient times. He considers going left but decides instead to move around the right side of the cairn, Lenox watching patiently as the King disappears from view behind the rock mound. It is early morning and very cold, Lenox lifting his hands from the reins to blow some warmth on them.

Macbeth hasn't gone far when he almost kicks over a little cage built from dozens of small, sun-bleached animal bones, with several tiny, bare skulls inside. Hearing a noise behind him suddenly, Macbeth wheels around, but no one is there. He turns back, but starts: Hecate's little girl is staring up at him, holding out a hand for him to take. He gazes at her: the white gown that reaches to the ground, the ring of white flowers she wears on her head, the long white hair and piercing blue eyes. She gestures impatiently for Macbeth to take her hand in his. So he does, and instantly finds himself walking in a pitch black space, the little girl hurrying him forward through the darkness, somewhere far ahead the faint sound of voices, chanting...

In the center of a dimly lit underground cave, the three black-cloaked witches are huddled around a fire over which they've hung a black, steaming cauldron. On the earth floor around them the organs, heads and limbs of animals, birds and reptiles are laid, some still wriggling.

"The tabby cat has meowed three times," the first witch cries.

"The hedgehog whined three times plus one," the second witch calls.

"Hecate cries, 'It's time, it's time!'" the third witch cackles, her words the signal for all three to join hands and circle the boiling pot.

"Round about the cauldron go," the first witch chants, "in it poisoned entrails throw. Toad, that under cold stone lay, thirty-one nights and days, slept while venom sweat oozed out: boil these first in the charmed pot!"

The others join in: "Double, double, toil and trouble; fire burn and cauldron bubble."

"Toss the meat of rattle snake," the second witch chants, "in the cauldron boil and bake: eye of newt and toe of frog, fur of bat and tongue of dog, adder's fork and blind-worm's sting, lizard's leg and young owl's wing, for a charm of lasting trouble, red-hot hell's broth boil and bubble."

Her sisters join in: "Double, double, toil and trouble, fire burn and cauldron bubble.

"Scale of dragon, tooth of wolf," the third witch chants, "witch's mummy, maw and gulf, of the savage salt-sea shark, root of hemlock dug at dark, liver of unholy Jew, gall of goat and twigs of yew, severed in the moon's eclipse, nose of Turk and Tartar's lips, thumb of babe that in a ditch, was born and strangled by a bitch; make the soup grow thick and clot: add tiger's guts to what we've got, for the mixture in our pot."

The other two join in: "Double, double, toil and trouble, fire burn and cauldron bubble."

"Cool it with a baboon's blood, then the spell is firm and good."

"Oh well done!" the voice of Hecate praises and she steps forward in her dark, hooded cloak. "I most approve of all your pains, and every one shall share the gains, so now about the cauldron sing, like elves and fairies in a ring, magic potion thus enchanting."

The second witch suddenly stops moving. " – By the pricking of my thumbs, something wicked this way comes."

"Open, locks," her sister says.

"Whoever knocks!" the third witch cries, and turns with the others to see the little girl and Macbeth emerging from the shadows, hand in hand.

"Now, you dark and midnight hags!" he roars, releasing the little girl's hand and charging forward, unafraid, to confront them by their black and steaming cauldron pot, "what is this evil magic that you do?"

"A deed without a name," the giddy witches grin.

"I beseech you, in the name of the black and secret art you practice, and however you come to know such things, answer me: though you unleash the winds that topple churches' steeples, foam the waves that batter and destroy men's sailing ships, crush the fields of ripening grain and forest trees blow down, crumple buildings on the heads of those who live within them, whirl about the pyramids until they wear away and sink down in the desert sand – though the very seeds of Nature tumble and fall together, even till destruction sickens itself, tell me what I need to know!"

"Speak."

"Demand."

"We'll answer."

"But tell us: would you hear it from our mouths or from our masters?"

"Call them. Let me see them," he says.

"Pour in pig's blood," the first witch chants, "sweet red juice of one who chewed her young; add the grease of gallows noose from a murderer who was hung – throw these in the flames!" She tosses a bowlful of blood under the fire and flames shoot up around the cauldron. "Come you spirits high and low – "

" – Ourselves!"

" – Our work!"

" – Deftly show!"

Off to one side, Hecate looks on, a silent but controlling presence. She flings open the folds of her cloak and a head wearing an armored helmet with the visor down is suddenly hovering in the air before Macbeth.

"Tell me, unknown power – "

"He knows your thoughts," the first witch scolds, "listen while he speaks but say nothing yourself."

"Macbeth, Macbeth, Macbeth," the First Spirit says in a low, warning voice, "beware Macduff, beware the Thane of Fife. Dismiss me. Enough." The head starts spinning...

"Whatever you are," Macbeth says quickly, "for your wise caution, thanks, you have marked my first fear well, but one more question – "

"He will not be commanded," the first witch calls.

Zph! The spinning spirit head is gone.

"Here's another, more potent than the first."

Hecate's cloak opens and a child covered face and body in fresh blood, staggers up to Macbeth and clings to his leg for dear life.

"Macbeth, Macbeth, Macbeth," the Second Spirit cries.

"If I had more ears, they would hear you."

"Be bloody," the child says coldly, "bold and resolute: laugh with scorn at the power of man, for no one born of woman shall harm Macbeth."

The child releases his leg and is whisked back to Hecate's cloak.

Zph!

"Then live, Macduff: what need I fear from you?" Macbeth rejoices. "And yet I'll make assurance double sure and take no chance with Fate: you shall not live, so I may laugh instead of fearing you and in despite of thunder, sleep the whole night through – "

Zph! The next thing Macbeth knows, a Third Spirit lies in his arms: a diapered baby, with a gold crown on its hairless head, a small fir tree in one of its hands.

"What is this?" he asks the witches, stupefied.

"Listen," they purr together, "but do not speak, Macbeth."

"Be lion-hearted, proud," the Third Spirit says in a fragile, soft voice, "and worry not who bothers or upsets you, or is hatching plots against you. Macbeth shall never be defeated until Great Birnam Wood shall come against him high on the hill of Dunsinane."

Zph! After the Third Spirit dissolves in Macbeth's arms and is gone, the crown is left resting in his hand. Perplexed, he holds it up, only to see it become a hissing snake that strikes and almost hits his face before he hurls it to the ground, where it slithers, hissing, away.

"Birnam Wood to climb the hill of Dunsinane? That will never be," Macbeth scoffs, "for who can move a forest, command a tree to pull up its roots and walk?" He smiles. "Joyous omens all! Good news!

Rebellious dead, never rise again till Birnam Wood rises? Then royal Macbeth shall live out his life until time and death, in mortal custom, have him take his final breath. Yet my heart throbs to know one thing: shall any of Banquo's descendants ever reign as king?"

"Seek to know no more."

"I demand to be told: deny me this, and may eternal curses fall on each of you. Let me know – "

As the cauldron begins to sink into the ground beneath the fire, Hecate waves one arm of her cloak and a vicious whistling wind begins to blow. A gesture with the other arm and a swath of burning flame flares along the cave floor.

"Why sinks the cauldron – what noise is this?" Macbeth shouts over the wind.

"Show!"

"Show!"

"Show!"

"Show his eyes," the witches chant, "and grieve his heart; come forth shadows, then depart…"

Within the flames closest to Macbeth, a king appears, blood flowing out from under his crown and dribbling down his face. A stream of birds comes pouring from his open mouth.

"You are like the spirit of Banquo – away! Your crown sears my eyes to their sockets."

The king continues to stand in the flames, a second appearing beside him, holding his chopped off head in his hands, the crown still in place.

"Your head is also crowned with gold – like the first…" Repulsed, he waves the apparition away and a third king appears, daggers protruding where his eyes should be, eyeballs skewered on the tips of the blades.

"This is like the others," Macbeth protests and turns on the witches. "Why show me this you filthy hags?"

Another king appears, the wind whistling in his face so hard the skin blows off and only the skeleton skull remains, still wearing its golden crown.

"A fourth? My eyes will burst!"

Hecate sweeps her cloak and whips the whistling wind to blow with such ferocity Macbeth is forced to clamp his hands upon his ears as a fifth and then a sixth king appear in rapid succession, each younger than the one before.

"What, will the line stretch to eternity?" he shouts over the wind.

A seventh king appears in the flames, younger still. His mouth moves but it's impossible to hear what he's saying.

" – Another yet? I'll see no more," Macbeth shrieks at the witches. "And now an eighth appears, a boy-king with a glass that shows me many like himself – and all of them the monarch's orb and scepter bear!" In the flames, the boy holds up his mirror and Macbeth cannot avert his eyes as the images of crowned kings continue to appear. "Horrible sight! Now I know it's true," he wails. "And blood-spattered Banquo smiles upon me, pointing to show these kings are his!"

Banquo's ghost steps out of the flames, with the boy-king, and together with the seven kings they move towards Macbeth.

"Say this is not so!" he cries.

Moving forward with Banquo and the seven kings, the boy holds up his mirror for Macbeth to watch as they close in and surround him, the kings removing their crowns and reaching to place them all upon his head – when Hecate sweeps the arm of her cloak:

Zph!

And the next instant Macbeth is lying on the ground outside the rock cairn, the Lord Lenox standing over him looking down, the sound of galloping horses not far away.

"Where are they?" Macbeth asks, confused.

Lenox frowns, not understanding.

"Gone?" Dazed, Macbeth sits up and looks around, the small cage built from animal bones at his feet. " – Let this pernicious hour be accursed forever in the calendar of my days," he says solemnly.

"What's your Grace's will?" Lenox asks, helping Macbeth up.

"You saw the Weird Sisters?"

"No, my Lord."

"They didn't pass by you?"

"No indeed, my Lord."

"May the air they ride on be infected, and all who trust them be damned!" He glances bitterly at the animal-bone cage beside the rocks, and without a second thought crushes it under his foot.

"I heard horses a moment ago," he says, stepping past Lenox. "Did they come by here?"

"Two or three men, my Lord," Lenox answers, following him around the cairn, "bringing word that Macduff has fled to England.

Macbeth stops before mounting his horse. "Fled to England?"

Lenox climbs on his horse. "Yes, my good Lord."

Macbeth waves him to go on ahead.

"Time anticipates the dreadful deeds at hand ," he says, retying a strap on his stirrup. "Decisions when arrived at must be acted on, or what's the use? If something comes to mind, it must be carried out at once or not all. And so first off, to turn ideas into deeds, no sooner will this thought be said than done: I will attack Macduff's castle without warning, seize Fife, and put to sword his wife, his children, and all unfortunate souls related to them. No boasting like a fool about it first; I'll do it when my temper's at its worst…and no more of these visions!" Mounting up, he calls ahead to Lenox. "Where are these gentlemen now?" Lenox points across the valley.

"Come, take me to them!"

They spur their horses to a gallop, and soon the witches' cairn is far behind…

On the garden lawn of Castle Fife it's a gray, windy afternoon, Lady Macduff looking on as Lord Rosse helps her young son practice his archery.

"What had he done to make him flee the country?" she wonders.

"You must be patient, madam," Rosse tells her, showing the boy a better way of gripping the arrow when he's pulling back the bowstring.

"He had none," Lady Macduff comes back. "Running away is madness! Our fears make us traitors, even if our actions don't," she adds.

"You don't know whether it was his wisdom or his fear that made him leave," Rosse says, watching the boy draw his bow, take aim and shoot, the arrow catching the outside edge of the straw target.

"Wisdom? To leave his wife, her children, his house and his possessions, in a place from which he himself has fled? He doesn't love us. He lacks in loving feeling to do this. Even the tiny wren will fight against the owl to protect the young ones in her nest. All this is from fear, and nothing about love – nor wisdom either. It goes against all reason for him to run."

Rosse turns to her. "My dearest cousin," he says patiently, "I ask you, please, to try and control your feelings. Your husband is a noble, wise and careful man who knows well the violence of these times. I dare not speak much more, except that these are difficult days when we can be called traitors without deserving it. Fear has us believing every rumor we hear, yet truly we do not know what it is we fear, and thus we float upon a wild and violent sea, tossed this way and that."

Shooting another arrow, the boy is discouraged when it hits the outside edge of the target again.

"I bid you goodbye for now," Rosse says gently, going over to her. "It won't be long before I'll come again. Let us hope for an end to these troubles before they get much worse. Blessing upon you, my pretty cousin." He and Lady Macduff embrace and kiss cheeks, just as young Macduff lets go an arrow that only narrowly misses the red cloth bull's eye. Shouting, he jumps for joy and looks to Rosse, who goes over and ruffles the boy's hair in congratulation. Rosse bends down and they hug, exchanging fond goodbyes, then he comes back to Lady Macduff.

"He has a father and yet he's fatherless," she comments, hurt tears brimming up in her eyes, but she refuses to start crying.

Moved, Rosse himself is close to tears. "I'm such a fool. If I stay longer I will disgrace myself and make you uncomfortable by letting you see me weep. I must leave."

He does, Lady Macduff turning to watch her son retrieve his arrows from the target, saving his near bull's eye for last.

"What will you do now your father's dead?" she calls. "How will you live?"

"As the birds do, mother."

"What, by eating worms and flies?"

"With whatever I can get, I mean, as they do."

Leaving his bow and arrows, he comes over to the stone bench where she has taken a seat.

"Poor bird!" she smiles and hugs him. "And you wouldn't be afraid of traps or snares?"

"Why should I, mother? They don't trap 'poor' birds. And he's not dead, my father, though you say he is."

"But he is, my boy. So what will you do for a father?"

"What will you do for a husband?" he turns the question back to her.

She laughs. "Why, I can buy myself twenty at any market."

"Then you'll buy them to sell again?"

"You speak like a child, but a clever one at that," she teases, tugging the gold medallion he wears on a chain around his neck: a gift from his father, from his father before him.

"Was my father a traitor, mother?"

"Yes, he was," she says.

The boy thinks for a moment. "What is a traitor?"

"Why, one who makes a vow but breaks it."

"And all who would do that, are they traitors?"

"Every one who does is a traitor and must be hanged."

"Must every one who breaks a vow be hanged?"

"Every one."

"Who must hang them?"

"Why, the honest men."

"Then the ones who break their vows are fools, for there must be enough of them to take the honest men out and hang them instead."

Lady Macduff smiles. "Well, God help you, poor monkey! But still, what will you do for a father?"

The boy shrugs. "If he were truly dead, you would weep for him. If you didn't weep, it would be a good sign that I would soon have a new father."

"My little chatterbox, how you talk!"

A female servant comes outside and shows a messenger across the lawn, Lady Macduff sending the boy back to his archery.

Restless and uneasy, the messenger presents himself. "Bless you fair lady," he begins quickly, "you don't know me, but I am well acquainted with your noble family. I fear some danger is soon approaching and, if you will take a plain man's advice, it will be best if you're not found here. Flee with your little ones. I feel cruel to be saying such a frightening thing, but to leave you in harm's way would be dangerous and much more cruel – and cruelty is all too near, I fear to say. Heaven protect you – I dare not stay longer." He turns and leaves, the servant running to keep up with him.

"Why would I flee?" she muses to herself. "I've done no harm. But after all, I am in this earthly world," she scoffs, "where doing harm is often praised, and doing good no more than foolishness. Why then even bother to say 'I've done no harm' in my own defense?" She shakes her head. "Whose faces are these?" she asks looking up.

Swords in hand, five men in the black attire of bandits push the frantic servant aside and march across the lawn, Lady Macduff remaining calm as the leader steps forward and takes her by the hair.

"Where is your husband?" he snaps.

"I hope in no place so dreadful that the likes of you might find him."

He sneers, showing silver teeth. "He's a traitor," he says with disdain.

"You lie, villain!" the boy calls, and releases one of his arrows. There's a *phht!* through the air and a quick, resounding *thung*! as it strikes the bandit in the upper thigh. A large man, he looks down at the arrow almost in amusement.

"What, you egg?" he roars, the other bandits rushing forward until the man holds out his sword to keep them at bay. He walks over to the boy, snapping the arrow off just above where it went in.

"No!" Lady Macduff cries and starts toward her son.

"Traitor's brat," the bandit says, and buries his sword in the boy's body.

In her frenzy, Lady Macduff trips and falls, screaming, to the ground.

"He has killed me, mother," the boy gasps in pain, "run, I beg you…"

The bandit puts a foot on the boy's bloody chest to pull his sword free, but spots the gold medallion and rips the chain from the boy's neck, turning to see Lady Macduff fleeing toward the castle, shrieking helplessly:

"Murder! Murder!"

The bandits are fast going after her, while their leader, a satisfied look on his face, tucks the gold medallion into his belt as he comes along behind....

Light from a late-afternoon autumn sun is golden on the spires of the great abbey at Westminster, where brown-robed monks comfort the sick and suffering as they wait to be received inside the church by King Edward the Confessor, while in the adjacent abbey park, the king's majestic swans glide placidly in the pond, Malcolm and Macduff drifting close by in a small wooden boat, deep in conversation.

"Let us find some dark and lonely place to weep until we can weep no more," Malcolm says. Looking discouraged, he gazes over the back of the boat into the water.

Macduff, at the oars, disagrees. "Let us take our battle swords instead, and like good men stand up and defend the land of our birth. Each new day new widows wail, new orphans cry, new sorrows strike at heaven's face so it echoes the grieving sound as if in sympathy with Scotland, and cries out in sorrow of its own."

"What I believe, I'll mourn; what I know, believe; what I can remedy, when the time is right, I will." Uneasy, Malcolm shifts in his seat. "What you have said may possibly be true. This tyrant, whose very name blisters our tongues, was once held to be honest: you loved him well. He has not injured you yet. I am young, but you could be working to win his favor by betraying me to him. It would not be unwise to sacrifice a weak, poor, innocent lamb to appease an angry god..."

"I am no traitor," Macduff comes back resentfully.

"But Macbeth is," Malcolm points out dejectedly. Several swans move peacefully past the boat. "Even a good and virtuous nature can give way before a king's command." He watches Macduff, whose head is bowed. "Yet I will beg your pardon: my suspicions cannot change that which you are one way or another. Angels are still bright even though Lucifer, brightest of all, fell…though truthfully, every evil thing tries to seem virtuous, while virtue's appearance does not change."

"I have lost hope then."

"Perhaps that is the source of my suspicions. Why did you leave unprotected your wife and children – those most precious to you, whom you love most – without saying farewell? I implore you, Macduff," Malcolm says earnestly, "don't see my suspicions as dishonoring you, but as all I have to protect myself. You may well be honorable, in spite of what I think."

"Bleed, bleed, poor country!" Macduff despairs. "Great tyranny, lay your foundations freely, for goodness dares not stop you. Wear what you have wrongly gained in safest satisfaction – your title to the crown confirmed as no one will oppose you!" Taking up the oars to begin rowing, he meets Malcolm's eyes. "Farewell, my Lord: I swear by the country that now lies in the tyrant's grasp, I am not the criminal you take me for."

"Do not be offended, I am not completely in distrust of you. Yes, I think our country sinks into bondage, weeping, bleeding, each day a new gash added to her wounds. Yet I also think that there are some who would fight for my cause. And here I have the offer of good men by the thousand from the gracious King of England. But even so, when I shall have the tyrant's head beneath my foot or planted on my sword, my poor country will have more vices than it had before. The man who succeeds Macbeth will have the country suffer more and differently than any one could know."

"Who will that be?" Macduff frowns, letting go the oars.

"I mean myself," Malcolm explains, "in whom the seeds of wickedness are so rooted that when they flower, black Macbeth will seem as pure as driven snow, the country remembering the lamb in him, compared with my boundless evil."

"Not in all the armies of horrible hell can there be a devil more damned in his evil than Macbeth."

"He's murderous, I grant, full of malice, greed, lechery, violence and deceit – guilty of every sin that has a name: but there's no end, none at all, to my own lechery: having your wives, your daughters, your married women and young maids, would never fill my appetite, never dry the springs of lust that in me flow, and my desire would overpower any virtuous force that did not bend to do my will. Better that Macbeth should rule than ever one like me."

"Unrestrained desire can tyrannize human nature, there is no question. It has brought an early end to many a happy throne and the downfall of many kings. But still you must not fear to take upon you what is yours: have that pleasure you crave in secret and meanwhile seem to the world still pure. You can deceive them: there are more than enough women willing to give themselves up to the hunger of their king."

"Though that may be, along with lust such constant greed is growing now within my evil heart, that if I were the King of Scotland I would kill the nobles for their lands, wanting this one's jewels and that one's house, and having a taste of this would provoke unjust quarrels against the good and loyal, destroying them for their wealth."

"This greed grows deeper: grows from roots more dangerous than those of youthful lust, and it has been the undoing of many a murdered king. Yet do not fear. Scotland has treasures by the trove that would satisfy your craving. These vices are most bearable, my Lord, when weighed against your virtues."

"But I have none," Malcolm protests, gazing toward the abbey. "The virtues that become a king such as justice, generosity, patience, courage, mercy and humility – there is no hint of them in me, but I am riddled with every kind of sin, and I act upon them in every way. No, if I had the power, I would dash all harmony to bits, throw peace into universal uproar, ruin all fellowship on earth."

"Oh Scotland, Scotland," Macduff laments.

"If someone like me is fit to govern, tell me: for I am exactly what I have described."

"Fit to govern – no, not so much as to live! Oh miserable nation, when will you see wholesome days again, free from a usurping tyrant's bloody rule, while the rightful heir to the throne stands condemned by self admission, and defiles his own ancestral line? Your royal father was a most saintly king; your mother the queen was more often on her knees in prayer than on her feet, prepared for death each day of her life. Farewell," he broods and begins rowing toward shore. "These evils you reveal about yourself have banished me from Scotland. Oh my heart, my hope ends here…" Macduff rows on in silence, the oars creaking in their locks.

Malcolm watches him thoughtfully for several moments, the boat drawing near the sand beach where some hounds are frisking in the shallow water.

"Macduff," he says, "this noble passion which is born of your integrity, has wiped the black suspicions from my soul and convinced me of your truth and honor. Devilish Macbeth has tried, through plots like this, to lure me to my death before; wise caution is what holds me back from believing too quickly whatever I am told. But as God above is our judge, from now on I will submit to your direction. I take back those disparaging words I used against myself just now, deny they are, or ever were, the truth. Indeed, I have yet not even had a woman, never broken an oath I've taken, barely felt desire for those things I own already. I have never been disloyal, would not betray the devil himself, to anyone, for gain, and I value truth as much as life itself. The first lie I ever told was what I said just now about myself. What I truly am is yours and my poor country's to command: indeed, before you came here, old Siward was eager to head for Scotland with ten thousand English soldiers – now we shall go together, and may our chance of success be equal to the justness of our cause!"

The boat glides into shore, Macduff racking the oars and stepping out of the boat.

"Why are you silent?" Malcolm asks, joining Macduff on the beach.

Macduff hesitates before answering. "It's hard to reconcile such contradictions all at once, my Lord…" He watches sullenly as a white-haired gentleman in a doctor's pale blue cap and robe hurries along beside the pond, more crutches in his arms than he can carry.

"Well, more of this shortly," Malcolm says to Macduff. He calls to the passing doctor. "Will the King be coming out soon?"

"Yes, sir," the doctor grins joyously, struggling to keep his load of crutches evenly balanced. "But still the most unfortunate invalids are waiting for his cure, those whose disease defeats the greatest efforts of all our medical men. But who, at the King's touch, return to health at once, such holiness has Heaven given his hand – " His final words come quickly and though he moves to keep his stack of crutches balanced, a few come loose and fall.

Malcolm goes and picks them up, sets them carefully back on top of the others. "Thank you, doctor."

"Thank you, sir," the doctor says, and continues on his way toward the abbey.

"What disease is this he mentions?" Macduff wonders.

"It's called the King's Evil. Often during my time in England I have seen the most miraculous healing from good King Edward. How he prevails upon heaven for aid, only he can say, but subjects afflicted with strange disease, their bodies swollen and covered in sores, pitiful to see and beyond all help of surgery, he is able to cure by hanging a gold medallion round their necks while he recites a holy prayer. And it is said he bequeaths this healing power to future kings: along with which he has the gift of heavenly prophecy, and the many blessings that have attended his reign bespeak his saintly grace."

Macduff nods, noticing the Lord Rosse making way to let the doctor pass. "Look who comes," he says to Malcolm.

"A countryman, though more than that I do not know him."

"My ever noble cousin," Macduff greets Rosse, "welcome."

"I recognize him now," Malcolm says and puts out his hand for Rosse to shake. "May God soon put an end to what keeps us strangers from each other."

"Amen, sir," Rosse agrees.

"Stands Scotland as it did?" Macduff inquires.

"Alas, the country is almost ashamed to see what it's become. It cannot be called our mother, but rather our grave, where none but those who know nothing can ever smile; where sighs and groans and shrieks that fill the air are hardly noticed now, and deepest sorrow is commonplace. People seldom ask for whom the funeral bell tolls, good men dying before the flowers in their caps do, as they die before there's even time to suffer sickness."

"This is painful to the ears," Macduff shakes his head, "but all too true," he says with a look to Malcolm.

"What's the latest sadness?" Malcolm questions Rosse.

Rosse gives a shrug. "Fresh news is old within the hour; each minute brings word of further grief."

"How is my wife?"

"Why, well."

"And all my children?"

"Well too."

"The tyrant has not shattered their peace?"

"No, they were at peace when I last saw them."

Something in Rosse's manner troubles Macduff. "Speak more freely if you would," he says bluntly, "how goes the struggle?"

Rosse meets his eyes uneasily. "When I came here bearing news that I have sadly delivered, a rumor was afoot that many worthy men had taken up arms against Macbeth, which I believe is true, for I saw the tyrant's forces on the march." He turns to Malcolm. "Now is the time to help. The moment you appear in Scotland, soldiers would spring up and our women too would fight to rid the country of its terrible misfortunes."

"Let them take comfort," Malcolm declares, "we are coming soon: the gracious King of England has lent us good Siward and ten thousand fighting men. There is not a better soldier in any land today."

"I wish I could with equal comfort answer," Rosse responds, "but I have words as well that should be howled out in the desert air, where they would not be heard."

"Who do these words concern?" Macduff asks. "Our general cause? Or is this sorrow for one person to know?"

"No heart that feels would shun this woe to share," Rosse says, "though it pertains to you alone, Macduff."

"If it is mine, don't keep it from me longer – tell me now."

Rosse struggles to break the news. "Let not your ears despise my tongue for bringing them the saddest sound that ever they will hear."

"No – " Macduff chokes at the thought, "I know what this is – "

"Your castle was taken by surprise, your wife and children savagely slaughtered: to tell you more of what occurred would add you to the heap of dead for hearing it would kill you."

"Merciful Heaven!" Malcolm exclaims, distraught.

Macduff trudges into the water up to his knees, bends over and with his cupped hands splashes water on his face to hide the rush of tears. Sobbing, he looks up to the sky.

After a moment, Malcolm enters the water, comes up behind Macduff and puts a hand on his shoulder.

"Don't hide these tears, sir," he says gently. "Give your sorrow words, for grief that does not speak, whispers to the overburdened heart and breaks it."

"My children too?"

Rosse nods. "Wife, children, servants, all who could be found."

"And I was not there. My wife killed too?"

"As I told you."

"Be comforted," Malcolm says, offering hope. "Let's make of our revenge the medicine that cures this terrible grief."

"He has no children," Macduff says. He turns to Rosse. "All my pretty ones? Did you say all?" Rosse nods gravely. "That vulture from hell. All, and their mother killed too, in one fell swoop…" Shaking his head in despair, Macduff looks away as he surrenders to his sorrow sobbing hard.

"Bear it like a man, sir," Malcolm says kindly.

"I will," Macduff accepts his words, "but I must also feel it like a man. I cannot but remember how precious these were to me." He glances at Malcolm. "Did heaven look on and do nothing to give them aid?" he demands and clenches his fists. "Macduff you sinner!" he shouts, and his voice echoes across the water. "They were killed because of you! Worthless as I am, they were slaughtered not for their misdeeds, but mine…" He stands for a moment, lost in thought. Finally he lets out a breath, composes himself and comes out of the water. " …May they rest in Heaven now."

"Let this be sharpening to your sword," Malcolm urges. "Let grief be changed to anger – let this enrage your heart, not break it."

"I could play the woman and weep, give vent to my fury in

boasting threats and angry curses. But gentle Heaven, cut short the least delay – bring this Scottish fiend unto my face. Set him within reach of my sword. If he escapes then, may heaven forgive him too…"

"Spoken like the man you are. Come, we will go to the King. Our power is ready, nothing remains to be done but take our leave. Macbeth is ripe for the picking, and angels above are set to guide us in the fray. Take what righteous comfort you may, the night is long that does not end in day…."

In the dead of night, all is quiet on the stairs and along the corridors of Dunsinane Castle, a lone torch burning beside the alcove where the royal doctor and a gentlewoman attending on Lady Macbeth have dozed off on their stools: the doctor with his head resting against the alcove wall, arms folded over his chest, his black instrument bag open on his knees, the gentlewoman's head slumped against his shoulder, hands folded in her lap. She has just made a sound and smiled at something in her dream, when a black cat pads slowly out of the surrounding darkness, its green eyes flashing briefly in the torchlight.

Eyeing the instrument bag and the two sleeping people, the cat prowls over, hops carefully onto the doctor's lap and peers inside the bag, spotting something which prompts it to dip an exploring paw inside – until the doctor stirs and smacks his lips. The cat pulls back its paw and freezes until silence resumes, going into the bag again after a few moments, but this time using both front paws to dig out what it wants, its weight on the edge of the open bag causing it suddenly to tip sideways, the cat jumping free a moment before the instrument bag falls noisily to the floor, spilling out its contents.

Startled awake, the doctor realizes what's happened and grumbles in complaint, nudging the gentlewoman beside him. She opens her eyes, glances immediately at the stairs across the way, then watches the doctor on his hands and knees, replacing the instruments, white bandage cloth, and a ball of string, in his bag, protesting that he's "too old for this sort of thing" until she whispers for him to be quiet and never mind.

"I've stayed awake with you for two nights now," he says, returning to his stool, "yet I've seen nothing that bears out what you've told me. How long has this…sleepwalking been going on?" he asks her.

"Ever since His Majesty went to war. She rises from her bed about this very time of night, wraps a blanket around her, unlocks a box she has, and takes out pen and paper. Folding it just so, she writes things down, reads the words to her self, seals the paper with wax, and then returns to her bed. Yet all the while she's fast asleep."

"Most disturbing," the doctor comments. "To experience the balm of sleep but at the same time behave as if she's wide awake…" He contemplates the matter for a moment. "During this agitated slumber, as it were, besides her walking and other manifestations as I would call them, are there things you have heard her say?"

"Nothing I can repeat, sir."

"You may tell me, madam, it's advisable that you do if I'm to offer any help."

"Not to you or anyone else," the gentlewoman says adamantly, "since there is no one who can confirm that what I heard and what she said are one and the same – look, sir, there she is!"

The doctor's eyes are agog: staring blindly, Lady Macbeth comes slowly down the stairs by the light of a candle she's holding, a blanket over rather than around her shoulders, but has nothing on underneath.

"This is her usual practice," the gentlewoman explains, "and I'm sure she's sound asleep. See for yourself, but stay out of sight, sir, lest we frighten her."

"How did she get the light?"

"It was by her bed: she keeps a burning candle with her through the night, she orders that it be so."

"You can see her eyes are open."

"Yes, but I know they see nothing."

"What is she doing now? Look how she rubs her hands…"

"It's a habit with her, to make the motion of washing her hands. I've known her to keep doing it for upwards of a quarter hour."

"But here's a spot," Lady Macbeth scolds. Reaching the bottom of the stairs, she sets the candle down and furiously scratches, more than rubs, the top of one of her wrists.

"Listen, she's talking," the doctor whispers, and digs quickly for something in his instrument bag. "I'll write down what she says so as to confirm my recollections later."

"Out damned spot!" Lady Macbeth cries miserably, scratching harder. "Out I say! – One, two: when now it's time to do it. Hell is murky. – Shame, my Lord, shame! A soldier, and afraid? Why should we fear who knows it, when no one can call us to account? – Yet who would have thought the old man to have so much blood in him?"

"Did you hear that?" the doctor whispers, taken aback.

"The Thane of Fife, had a wife: where is she now? – What, will these hands never be clean? – No more of that, my Lord, no more of that: you ruin everything if you panic."

"Dear, dear," the doctor murmurs to the gentlewoman, "you know things that you shouldn't…"

"Because she has said things she shouldn't have, I'm sure of that. Heaven only knows what they must be..."

Lady Macbeth brings her wrists up to her nose and sniffs. "The smell of blood is still there: all the perfumes of Arabia would not sweeten this little hand. Oh! Oh!! Oh!!!" she cries in desperation.

"What agony she's in," the doctor observes, "her heart is in torment."

"I wouldn't have it in my breast even if I were a queen."

"Well, well, well…" The doctor heaves a troubled sigh.

"Pray God things will be, sir," the gentlewoman says hopefully.

"This disease is beyond my practice: though I have known some who walked in their sleep to die peacefully in their beds."

"Wash your hands," Lady Macbeth says in a hushed whisper, "put on your dressing gown. Don't look so worried. – I tell you once again, Banquo's dead and buried: he cannot come back from the grave…"

"Is that what happened then?" The doctor turns to the gentlewoman, who shrugs.

"To bed, to bed!" Lady Macbeth says in a panic, "there's knocking at the gate! Come, come, come, come, give me your hand. What's done is done. To bed, to bed, to bed…" She picks up the candleholder and ascends the stairs, the doctor watching as the flickering candle moves off down the corridor above, and disappears.

"Will she go to bed now?"

"Right away," the gentlewoman nods.

A dip of the quill in his inkpot, the doctor scribbles a final note to himself. "No wonder vicious rumors are about," he frowns. "'Unnatural acts," he reads aloud what he's writing, "'can't help but cause unnatural trouble. Sick minds, will confess their secrets to their deaf pillows.'" Done, he deposits his paper, pen and ink in the instrument bag. "She needs a priest more than a doctor," he declares grimly. " – God, God, forgive us all!" he laments as he closes up his bag. "Look after her, and take away whatever she could use to hurt herself, but still keep an eye on her," he advises. " – So, good night: she has me confounded, I will say that. I wouldn't believe it if I hadn't seen this myself." He shakes his head. "I don't dare say what I think…"

"Good night, good doctor."

Together they gaze over at the stairs one final time before heading off along the corridor….

A light snow is falling as the armies of Scotland gather where the country road bends around three ancient oak trees, their branches now bare, soldiers under the command of the nobles Menteth and Caithness marching in two columns along the road, as troops commanded by the lords Angus and Lenox come from all directions through the surrounding fields to join their countrymen on the march toward Dunsinane, where they will lay siege to Macbeth's castle. In both contingents there are many young faces: boys proud, excited and…terrified to be going to war for the first time.

Angus and Lenox reaching the road, where the marching columns have just received orders to stand easy until their allies have joined up with them, the two nobles ride quickly up the line to confer with Menteth and Caithness, their men cheering the admired lords as they pass.

"The English force is close by," Menteth announces, greeting Angus and Lenox, "and is led by Malcolm, his uncle Siward and the good Macduff. Revenge burns in them with such vehemence, after the unspeakable wrongs they have suffered at the hands of Macbeth, that the dead, the halt and the maimed would gladly take up arms in this grim call to battle."

"They're coming past Birnam Wood. I'm told we will meet them there," Angus reports.

"Do we know if Donalbain is with his brother?" Caithness wonders.

"It seems not," Lenox answers. "I have a list of our nobles, which includes Siward's son and many young men who are bearing arms for the first time, but his name is not among these."

"How is the tyrant likely to proceed against us?" Menteth asks.

"He has strongly fortified Dunsinane," Lenox says. "Some say he's gone mad. Others, who hate him less, say he has put himself into a 'valiant fury.'" This draws an uneasy chuckle from the other lords. "But one thing is certain: he cannot sustain a prolonged siege if he has succumbed to a derangement that robs him of his self-control."

"He has much blood on his hands," Angus submits. "Perhaps his secret murders have come back to haunt him. More revolt against his treasonous rule every day. Those he commands only obey him out of fear, not loyalty. No doubt he feels his title too big for him: a giant's robe on a wee thief." At this there is uncomfortable laughter all round.

"Who could blame him for being tormented by feelings of fear and loathing," Menteth says, "when he knows so much within him condemns itself for being there."

"Well, we march on to give obedience where it's due," Caithness declares. "Let us meet Malcolm and with him pour everything we have, down to the last drop of blood, into ridding our land of this disease."

"Or as much as is needed to help the new king flower," Lenox adds, "drowning the weeds that have flourished untended for too long. On to Birnam."

"Bring me no more reports!" Macbeth rages in his private dining chamber, and swipes the iron poker in his hand so the hooked point slashes the cheek of a servant who has just delivered the news that thanes loyal to him until now have gone over to the enemy side. Clutching his bleeding face, the hapless servant retreats to the door, where the doctor takes him aside and tends to the open wound, while Macbeth goes back to stirring remnants of a fire in the hearth which has all but gone out.

"Let them all desert me!" he rails defiantly, "I have nothing to fear till Birnam Wood comes to Dunsinane. Who is this boy Malcolm? Was he not born of woman? Spirits that foretell the future have told me this: 'Fear not, Macbeth, no man who's been born of woman shall ever have power over you!' Flee if you like, false thanes, and join the English dandies. For a will as firm and a heart as fierce as mine will not be swayed nor cower in fear before any of you."

Another servant enters and advances, petrified, bringing a message to the King.

"Let the devil damn you, pale-faced loon! Where do you get such a look, goose?"

"There are ten thousand – "

"Geese, fool?"

"Soldiers, sir," the servant says meekly.

"Go pinch your face till some red comes into it, rub some blood from the weakling there to hide your fear while you're at it, you timid sot. What soldiers, fool?" The servant shakes, terrified. "Damn you! You want those white cheeks to get us all shivering in our boots? What soldiers, you ninny?"

"The English army, so please you."

"Get out of my sight!"

The servant turns and races for the door, the doctor throwing him a commiserating glance as he sends the first servant on his way at the same time.

"Seyton!" Macbeth shouts and flings the poker away in disgust. He places both hands over the fireplace and stares down at the smoldering coals. "I am sick at heart when I behold – " He breaks off. "Seyton, I say! The outcome here will see my reign live on for good or unseat me now." He pauses, his mood shifting. "I have lived long enough, he says wistfully, "my life begins to wither, entering its yellow autumn, and that which should accompany old age – honor, love, obedience, troops of friends – I can never expect to have. But instead I'll know the curses – not spoken out loud but heartfelt nonetheless – and the lip-service of lackeys, which only the vain and weak of spirit would dare to deny, if even they could."

Seyton, an officer serving directly under the King, comes in quickly and presents himself.

"What is your gracious pleasure, Majesty?"

"Is there news?"

"None but that what has been reported to you so far is confirmed, my Lord."

"I'll fight, till my flesh is hacked from my bones. Give me my armor."

"It is not needed yet, Sire."

"I'll wear it. Send out more horsemen. Scour the surrounding countryside. Hang anyone who even mentions being afraid. Give me my armor," he demands again.

Seyton bows smartly and leaves, Macbeth turning to the doctor.

"How is your patient, doctor?"

"She is not so much sick, my Lord, as plagued by fierce imaginings that keep her from sleep."

"Cure her of that. Can you not help a sick mind? Pluck a deep-bedded sorrow from within her memory? Purge the heart of its unhappy burdens with some potion that brings on sweet oblivion?"

"In these things," the doctor replies sagely, "the patient must help himself." He meets the King's eyes with his own as Seyton returns with two attendants bearing Macbeth's armor.

"Throw medicine to the dogs," Macbeth scoffs, "I'll have none of it." He turns to Seyton. "Come, my armor," he says, and the attendants begin fitting the King's breastplate first, then his leg and arm protectors. He motions for his sword and belt, but pauses before buckling it on. "My spear as well," he tells Seyton, who nods and makes for the door. "Send out more men," he calls after his officer, catching the doctor's eye. "Doctor, my thanes are abandoning me." At a loss as to how he should respond, the doctor shakes his head in apparent disapproval and frowns. "Hurry, sir!" Macbeth shouts impatiently, sighing as he fastens on his sword. "If you could examine my country, doctor, find her disease and make her as sound and healthy as she once was, my praise would go out to you and I would applaud your efforts with vigor," he says as though he means it. He moves about the room in his heavy armor, clearly uncomfortable, the attendants watching him apprehensively. "Take it off!" he orders, changing his mind just as Seyton returns with the eight-foot long spear. Utterly afraid, the attendants waste no time removing the various pieces of armor promptly. "What herb or flower, what drug would cleanse us of these English, good doctor? Have you heard about them?"

"Yes, my good lord. Your Majesty's preparations have made us aware of them."

"Have them follow me with it," Macbeth instructs Seyton. With his armor off, he goes to a massive sideboard off to one side of the room, where numerous plates of uneaten food are precariously stacked. He bends over, uses a key and opens a lower drawer from which he takes a small wooden chest. "This too," he informs Seyton, who marches over and accepts it from the King.

On his way to the door, Macbeth stops beside the doctor. He stops, and has Seyton open the box. Macbeth reaches in and takes out a handle of gold coins. "I will not be afraid of death or pain," he smirks at the doctor, "till Birnam Wood comes to Dunsinane." He takes the doctor's hand and places the gold coins in his palm.

But the moment the others are gone, the doctor walks straight to the fireplace and tosses the money in the ashes. "No sum of money can hold me here," he says bitterly, turns for the door and leaves....

With drums beating, officers on horseback shouting orders to the infantry and the siege fighters rolling catapults, grappling ladders and battering rams into position, the armies of Scotland and England are massing in the broad field adjacent to a forest thick with spruce and fir trees. Malcolm, Siward, his young son, and Macduff oversee the English side; Lenox, Rosse, Menteth, Angus and Caithness the Scots.

"Cousins," Malcolm says, addressing the gathered nobles, "I hope the time is at hand when we will sleep safe in our homes."

"We are not doubting it for a moment, Sire," Menteth declares fervently.

"What forest is this in front of us?" Siward asks.

"Birnam Wood it is known as," Menteth tells him.

Malcolm has noticed one of his officers deploying troops with battle-axes to chop down trees along the edge of the road so the siege equipment will be able to pass. He gazes at Dunsinane Castle high on a hill in the distance.

"Have every soldier provided with a branch from the forest to carry in front of him: this will conceal the size of our force and have scouts relay mistaken reports to the tyrant about our numbers."

"It shall be done," says Malcolm's attending officer, hastening off to see that the order is executed.

"We hear nothing except that the tyrant, in his supreme confidence, yet remains in Dunsinane and will not try to prevent us from laying siege," Siward comments.

"It's all he can do," Malcolm responds, "his officers and men are deserting at every opportunity. Only those who are forced to at the point of a sword will serve under him now, which is hardly sufficient loyalty for an army defending its king against rebellion and enemy attack."

"Let us wait to pass judgment," Macduff advises, "until the outcome is decided. In the meantime, let us be the best soldiers we can."

"The time is near," Siward concurs, "when we will know the difference between what we hope to achieve, and what we truly can. Speculation but concerns itself with our hopes; victory must be won on the battlefield – yonder, on Dunsinane's slopes!"

Still without his armor, Macbeth moves among his officers and soldiers in the throne room at Dunsinane, Seyton following behind with the chest of gold coins.

"Hang out our banners on the outward walls," Macbeth proclaims in a rousing voice, "and remember, the signal to begin is still 'They're coming!' He greets one soldier after another, rugged louts who have the look of the mercenary about them, Seyton dutifully placing a gold coin in the King's hand, which he hands over to each man in turn, none of whom, judging by their astonished looks, has ever seen this much money before.

Soon he stops moving and takes in the faces gathered around him. "Our castle's strength will laugh in scorn at this siege," he says with disdain, "let the enemy sit here till famine and fever eat them up!" Amused, the soldiers laugh and mutter scoffing comments. "If they were not reinforced with those who have deserted us," he carries on, "we might have met them face to face on the open field and beat them back where they came from."

Approaching a group of men in the black attire of bandits, Macbeth orders Seyton to give each man extra, which prompts an appreciative smile from their leader, who instead of teeth along the top of his mouth has crude lumps of silver. Macbeth notices the gold chain and medallion he wears around his neck. Taking a closer look, he smiles. Without being asked, the man lifts off the chain and is handing the medallion to Macbeth when a woeful wailing can be heard in the corridor outside the room.

"What is that noise?"

"Women crying my Lord," Seyton replies. He gives Macbeth the chest of gold and hurries from the room. With the women's cries worsening, all eyes are trained questioningly on the King, who looks absently at the unfamiliar faces around him as he drifts back to the throne, murmuring to himself. "I have almost forgotten the taste of fear… Time was, a shriek in the night would make me shiver; and my hair would stand on end, as though it were alive, after a dark, murdering story…" He reaches the throne and sits, the chest of gold on his lap. "I have had my fill of horrors, the worst things imaginable… Yet, even the most heinous thoughts no longer startle me…"

Seyton comes back and approaches the throne. "The Queen is dead, my Lord," he reports grimly.

Keeping his eyes ahead, Macbeth stares at something across the room. As the King's face is without expression, Seyton gauges that he wants to be left alone and starts motioning for the officers and soldiers to depart.

"No," Macbeth blurts. "She would have died sooner or later," he says stoically. "One day, word would have come that it was so." On their way out, the soldiers look to Seyton. Sensing that the King has more to say, he turns and listens. The others do the same. " – Tomorrow, and tomorrow, and tomorrow creeps at its dismal pace, forward from day to day until the end of time, the yesterdays of memory a light that fools take with them to their graves. Out, out brief candle!" he says bitterly, "the living are but walking shadows, poor actors who strut and struggle in their simple parts upon the stage, and then are heard no more: life is a tale told by an idiot, full of sound and fury, but signifying nothing."

A messenger darts into the room and makes for the throne.

"You come to tell me something," Macbeth says as the man bows. "Give it quickly."

"My gracious Lord, I must report what I have seen, but don't know how to do it."

"Well, try, sir."

"Standing watch upon the castle hill, I looked toward Birnam and it appeared as if the woods themselves were moving."

"Liar!"

"Let me incur your anger, Sire, if this was not so, but you can see the forest moving, not three miles away."

"If you have made this up I will hang you alive on the closest tree and let you starve to death. If it is, I would not care if you did the same to me." He dismisses the man, gets up from the throne, and regards the room full of faces watching him. "My resolution falters," he confesses. "I begin to doubt those tricks the devil plays to make lies seem like truth. 'Fear not, till Birnam Wood comes to Dunsinane'," he scoffs, " – and now the woods are coming here to Dunsinane... To arms!" he explodes. "To arms, and into the field of battle!" A rousing cheer goes up throughout the room, Macbeth reflecting to himself beneath the noise: "If what he says is true, to stay or flee is all the same. I begin to be weary of the sun, and wish my time in the world were done. Sound the alarm!" he shouts to his men. "Start to beat the battle drum! Blow, wind! Destruction come! We'll not from thieving enemies run!"

And a cheer goes up throughout the room, for Macbeth, who is himself again....

Shoulder to shoulder, the archers atop the walls of Dunsinane fire waves of flaming arrows at the trees borne by English and Scottish soldiers as they come ever closer to the castle, drums beating, flags flying and banners streaming behind their advancing evergreen wall, where the arrows have now had their desired effect, fire spreading quickly so the soldiers cannot hold their branches much longer.

"This is near enough!" Malcolm shouts to his officers. "Have your men throw their branches down and show themselves as they are."

Spurring their horses, the officers charge along the line to relay the command, and within minutes the green forest is gone, but fifteen thousand soldiers are standing in its place.

Malcolm turns to Siward and his son. "You, worthy uncle, shall with my cousin, your noble son, lead the first assault. Worthy Macduff, we and the rest, shall follow up behind, according to our plan, attacking wherever openings can be found."

"Farewell," Siward nods and strikes a closed fist against his heart in salute. " – We venture forth against the tyrant's ruthless might, but let us be defeated if, to a man, we give it not our best and fiercest fight."

"Make our trumpets speak!" Macduff commands, "and blow with mightiest breath a clamoring that announces blood and death."

In the deafening blare of trumpets sounding the attack, Siward, his son and the English troops advance toward the castle walls ahead....

Shields held high to protect against the arrows raining down from above, Siward and his men are inside the castle yard, where all is pandemonium now that the battle has begun in earnest: the soldiers of Dunsinane giving way before the English onslaught, though not without a savage and brutal fight, while across the way, Macbeth's vicious sword-work keeps a dozen English soldiers at bay on a staircase leading up the side of the castle's inner wall.

"They have tied me to the stake. I cannot flee, but like a baited bear must fight unto the end. Where is the man not born of woman?" he shouts defiantly over the fray. "I am to fear that man or none at all!"

Soon, young Siward has fought his way up the stairs until it is his turn to stand before Macbeth.

"What is your name?" he demands.

"You will be afraid to hear it."

"No, not even if you called yourself the most hated name in Hell."

"I am Macbeth."

"The devil himself could speak no name more hateful to my ear."

"No, nor more frightening."

"You lie, loathsome tyrant! I'll prove that you lie with this sword – "

He attacks, cutting Macbeth in the arm above his elbow with the second swing of his sword. Amused, Macbeth lets the fight continue for a moment before he beats down the young man's sword and in a fierce, quick stroke, sticks his blade in young Siward's throat, and pitches him off the stairs, blood spraying from the body as it flies through the air to land in a wagon filled with burning hay.

"You were born of woman!" Macbeth yells and mounts to the top of the stairs. "I laugh with scorn at weapons brandished by men who are born of women!" He surveys the battle raging in the yard below then charges to an open door and disappears inside.

Moments after, Macduff takes cover beside the burning wagon to avoid a bevy of whizzing arrows targeted on him. "The noise is this way. – Tyrant, show your face!" he cries. "If you've been killed but with no sword of mine, my wife's and children's ghosts will haunt me ever after."

He decides to make a run for the stairs, though as he climbs he has to hack and stab his way through a half dozen soldiers in the black armor of bandits, their grinning leader falling to the fury of Macduff's relentless sword: his head lopped from his body so it bumps from stair to stair until it thuds on the ground at the bottom, a silver-toothed grin still twitching on its lips.

"I cannot fight these hired men who only fight for pay," Macduff sneers in disdain. "Either I find you, Macbeth, or my sword I put away – " A roar goes up across the yard. "You must be there, where the noise announces someone greater in rank than all the rest." Arrows hissing all around him, he leaps from the stairs, lands and heads toward a crowd of soldiers closing in on enemy quarry, Siward, arriving at the top of the stairs, watching him go until he spots Malcolm running up by the burning wagon.

"Behind you, my Lord!" Siward calls and jumps at the man about to plant his battle-axe in Malcolm's back. The man goes down beneath old Siward, who rolls free in time for Malcolm to run the axe-man through with his sword.

"We've taken the castle with barely a fight," Siward says, getting back on his feet. "The tyrant's men were surrounded – your nobles have fought their bravest, my Lord, our victory now appears certain, so there is little left to do."

Malcolm's troubled gaze is on the face of the man he has just killed.

"I have fought enemies that once fought beside me," he mourns.

Siward looks down at the dead man then meets Malcolm's eyes. "Enter the castle, Sir," he says plainly, stepping back to let Malcolm precede him up the stairs through clouds of smoke that are billowing up from the burning wagon of hay....

Out of breath and bloody from his wounds, Macbeth stops and leans against the wall in a corridor of the castle.

"Why should I play the defeated Roman and die upon my sword?" he asks himself. "While enemies live, the wounds are better received by them – "

"Turn, hellhound, turn!" Macduff cries and charges him from behind.

They skirmish briefly, Macduff stepping back when he notices the gold medallion Macbeth is wearing on a chain around his neck.

"You I have avoided more than any other," Macbeth confesses, "for my soul is too much burdened with the blood already shed within your family."

"I have nothing to say to you," Macduff sneers, glaring at the medallion. "My voice is in my sword, you bloodier villain than mere words can describe."

He swings his sword and goes after Macbeth, their weapons clashing in a violent fight with neither giving any quarter along the hall or in the atrium where they continue. "Give up, sir," Macbeth taunts, "you might as well try wounding the air with your keen blade as make me bleed. Let your blows fall on one who can be wounded – I lead a charmed life and cannot be taken down by anyone born of woman."

"Forget your charms, sir," Macduff comes back, "and let the sorcerer you serve relay the news: Macduff was prematurely ripped from his dear mother's womb."

"Cursed be the tongue that tells me this, for it strips me of my courage!" Macbeth says, distraught, but carries on the fight. "Believe no more in deceiving fiends who double deal their truth," he says about the witches, "keeping the words of promise they made, but denying us what we hoped for." He unleashes a fury of punishing blows that drives Macduff back toward a staircase, unaware that Seyton's body is sprawled on the floor behind him, his dead hands clutching the spear that went through his chest. Tripping, Macduff goes down, his sword sliding away. "I will not fight you more," Macbeth says, and makes for the stairs that rise to the floor above.

"Then surrender, coward!" Macduff calls after him, "and live to be the show and spectacle of our day! We'll have you, as our rarer monsters are, chained up to a pole, and on the sign will be the words: 'Here you see the tyrant.'

Macbeth stops at the top of the stairs and turns. "I will not deign to kiss the ground before young Malcolm's feet, nor let myself be mocked by jeering, rabble throngs. Birnam Wood has come to Dunsinane and I am facing you, who was not born of woman, yet I will fight until the last breath leaves my body. So, come Macduff, and damned be him who first cries 'Stop, enough!'"

Macduff retrieves his sword and pulls the spear from Seyton's body, but when he turns to face Macbeth, the King is no longer there....

The battle for the castle won, the soldiers of England and Scotland are streaming into Dunsinane: rounding up enemy prisoners, dousing fires the enemy set when they knew they were defeated, helping the walking wounded and loading stretchers with the dead, who are carefully borne to the wagons waiting beyond the castle yard. Siward and Rosse are walking with Malcolm, who greets the lords and thanes appearing in the yard, though his face registers concern for those he has yet to see.

"I wish our missing friends were here among us," he worries.

"Some must be dead," Siward says bluntly, "and yet from what we see so far, our victory has been cheaply bought."

"Macduff is unaccounted for, as is your son," Malcolm says to Siward.

"Your son, my lord, has died a soldier's death," Rosse speaks up. "He didn't get to be a man for long, I know. No sooner had his valor been confirmed – I'm told he stood his ground against the foe – than like a man he died."

"Then he is dead?" Siward asks.

"Yes, sir. Carried from the battlefield a very hero in the fight." Siward turns his face away. "Your grief must not be measured by his worth," Rosse says and puts a hand on Siward's shoulder. "For then it would have no end."

Siward nods, still with his back to Rosse. "Were his wounds in front?"

"They were, sir, in the front."

"Why, then," Siward allows, "he's God's soldier now. If I had as many sons as I have hairs upon my head, I could not wish them a better death than this."

"He's worth our greater sorrow, uncle," Malcolm says, "and I will see that it is shown."

"He's worth no more," Siward shakes his head. "They say he parted well and paid his score: so God be with him now. But look, here comes a newer comfort…"

Macduff appears on the landing overhead, Macbeth's head stuck on the point of his battle spear. Hurt and limping, the gold medallion around his neck, he makes his way to the top of the stairs and thrusts his spear in the air, for all to see.

"Hail, King, for so your are! See where the tyrant's cursed head now sits!" A roar goes up from the soldiers in the yard, Macduff hurling the spear into a fire burning down below, which prompts an even louder cheer. "Our lives are free of tyranny," he shouts, "and I see you surrounded by the finest men throughout this kingdom, whose voices will rise aloud with mine to greet you King of Scotland!"

"Hail, King of Scotland!" the soldier voices cry as one.

All eyes on the King, Malcolm mounts the first few stairs to speak. "We will not waste time in reckoning repayment for the loyalty you've shown. Henceforth, my thanes and kinsmen, I dub you Earls of Scotland, the first such honor ever there has been. What also must be done, in this our new established reign, is call our friends in exile home from other lands, who fled to save themselves from ruthless tyranny. We will bring to trial the henchmen of this dead, butcher king and his fiendish Queen – who it is said brought violence upon her self, and ended her own life. These things, and whatever else we're called upon to do, we will, by the grace of God, perform in proper measure, time, and place. So thanks to each and every one, whom we invite to see us crowned at Scone."

The cheer is loud and long that rises in the air to the ramparts high above, where a flag is now flying the colors royal, of Malcolm, King of Scotland….

New Directions

The Young and the Restless: *Change*
The Human Season: *Time and Nature*
Eyes Wide Shut: *Vision and Blindness*
Cosmos: *The Light and The Dark*
Nothing But: *The Truth in Shakespeare*
Relationscripts: *Characters as People*
Idol Gossip: *Rumours and Realities*
Wherefore?? *The Why in Shakespeare*
Upstage, Downstage: *The Play's the Thing*
Being There: *Exteriors and Interiors*
Dangerous Liaisons: *Love, Lust and Passion*
Iambic Rap: *Shakespeare's Words*
P.D.Q.: *Problems, Decisions, Quandaries*
Antic Dispositions: *Roles and Masks*
The View From Here: *Public vs. Private Parts*
3D: *Dreams, Destiny, Desires*
Mind Games: *The Social Seen*
Vox: *The Voice of Reason*

The Shakespeare Novels

Spring 2006

Hamlet
King Lear
Macbeth
Midsummer Night's Dream
Othello
Romeo and Juliet
Twelfth Night

Spring 2007

As You Like It
Measure for Measure
The Merchant of Venice
Much Ado About Nothing
The Taming of the Shrew
The Tempest

www.crebermonde.com

Shakespeare Graphic Novels

Fall 2006

Hamlet
Macbeth
Othello
Romeo and Juliet

www.shakespearegraphic.com

Paul Illidge is a novelist and screenwriter who taught high school English for many years. He is the creator of *Shakespeare Manga*, the plays in graphic novel format, and author of the forthcoming *Shakespeare and I*. He is currently working on *Shakespeare in America*, a feature-film documentary. Paul Illidge lives with his three children beside the Rouge River in eastern Toronto.